Tecumseh

CHARLES MAIR

Published in 1868

TABLE OF CONTENTS

MOTTO
DRAMATIS PERSONAE
ACT I. TECUMSEH
ACT II. TECUMSEH
ACT III. TECUMSEH
ACT IV. TECUMSEH

MOTTO

"When the white men first set foot on our shores, they were hungry; they had no places on which to spread their blankets or to kindle their fires. They were feeble; they could do nothing for themselves. Our fathers commiserated their distress, and shared freely with them whatever the Great Spirit had given to his red children."
From TECUMSEH'S speech to the Osages.

DRAMATIS PERSONAE

INDIANS:
TECUMSEH (Chief of the Shawanoes).
THE PROPHET (Brother of Tecumseh).
TARHAY (A Chief in love with Iena).
STAYETA (Chief of the Wyandots).
MIAMI, DELAWARE, KICKAPOO and DAHCOTA CHIEFS. Warriors, Braves, Josakeeds and Runners.
MAMATEE (Wife of Tecumseh).
IENA (Niece of Tecumseh).
WEETAMORE, WINONA and other Indian Maidens.
AMERICANS:
GENERAL HARRISON (Governor of Indiana Territory).
GENERAL HULL.
COLONEL CASS.
BARRON (An Indian Agent).
TWANG, SLAUGH, GERKIN and BLOAT (Citizens of Vincennes).
Five Councillors of Indiana Territory, Officers, Soldiers, Volunteers, Orderlies and Scouts.
BRITISH AND CANADIANS:
GENERAL BROCK (Administrator of the Government of Upper Canada).
COLONEL (afterwards General) PROCTOR. GLEGG, MACDONELL, Aides-de-camp to General Brock.
NICHOL, BABY, ELIOTT, Colonels of Canadian Volunteers.
McKEE, ROBINSON, Captains of Canadian Volunteers.

LEFROY (A poet-artist, enamoured of Indian life, and in love with IENA.)
Two Old men of York, U. E. Loyalists, and other Citizens, Alien Settlers, Officers, Soldiers, Volunteers, Orderlies and Messengers.

ACT I. TECUMSEH

SCENE FIRST.
THE FOREST NEAR THE PROPHET'S TOWN ON THE TIPPECANOE.

Enter the PROPHET.
PROPHET. Twelve moons have wasted, and no tidings still!
Tecumseh must have perished! Joy has tears
As well as grief, and mine will freely flow—
Sembling our women's piteous privilege—
Whilst dry ambition ambles to its ends.
My schemes have swelled to greatness, and my name
Has flown so far upon the wings of fear
That nations tremble at its utterance.
Our braves abhor, yet stand in awe of me,
Who ferret witchcraft out, commune with Heaven,
And ope or shut the gloomy doors of death.
All feelings and all seasons suit ambition!
Yet my vindictive nature hath a craft,
In action slow, which matches mother-earth's:
First seed-time—then the harvest of revenge.
Who works for power, and not the good of men,
Would rather win by fear than lose by love.
Not so Tecumseh—rushing to his ends,
And followed by men's love—whose very foes
Trust him the most. Rash fool! Him do I dread,
And his imperious spirit. Twelve infant moons
Have swung in silver cradles o'er these woods,

And, still no tidings of his enterprise,
Which—all too deep and wide—has swallowed him.
And left me here unrivalled and alone.
Enter an INDIAN RUNNER.
Ha! There's a message in your eyes—what now?
RUNNER. Your brother, great Tecumseh, has returned,
And rests himself a moment ere he comes
To counsel with you here.
[Exit Runner.]
PROPHET. He has returned!
So then the growing current of my power
Must fall again into the stately stream
Of his great purpose. But a moment past
I stood upon ambition's height, and now
My brother comes to break my greatness up,
And merge it in his own. I know his thoughts—
That I am but a helper to his ends;
And, were there not a whirlpool in my soul
Of hatred which would fain ingulf our foes,
I would engage my cunning and my craft
'Gainst his simplicity, and win the lead.
But, hist, he comes! I must assume the role
By which I pander to his purposes.
Enter TECUMSEH.
TECUMSEH. Who is this standing in the darkened robes?
PROPHET. The Prophet! Olliwayshilla, who probes
The spirit-world, and holds within his ken
Life's secrets and the fateful deeds of men.
The "One-Eyed!" Brother to the Shooting Star—
TECUMSEH. With heart of wax, and hands not made for war.
PROPHET. Would that my hands were equal to my hate!
Then would strange vengeance traffic on the earth;
For I should treat our foes to what they crave—
Our fruitful soil—yea, ram it down their throats,
And choke them with the very dirt they love.
'Tis you Tecumseh! You, are here at last,
And welcome as the strong heat-bearing Spring
Which opens up the pathways of revenge.
What tidings from afar?
TECUMSEH. Good tidings thence.
I have not seen the Wyandots, but all
The distant nations will unite with us

To spurn the fraudful treaties of Fort Wayne.
From Talapoosa to the Harricanaw
I have aroused them from their lethargy.
From the hot gulf up to those confines rude,
Where Summer's sides are pierced with icicles,
They stand upon my call. What tidings here?
PROPHET. No brand has struck to bark our enterprise
Which grows on every side. The Prophet's robe,
That I assumed when old Pengasega died—
With full accord and countenance from you—
Fits a strong shoulder ampler far than his;
And all our people follow me in fear.
TECUMSEH. Would that they followed you in love!
Proceed! My ears are open to my brother's tongue.
PROPHET. I have myself, and by swift messengers,
Proclaimed to all the nations far and near,
I am the Open-Door, and have the power
To lead them back to life. The sacred fire
Must burn forever in the red-man's lodge,
Else will that life go out. All earthly goods
By the Great Spirit meant for common use
Must so be held. Red shall not marry white,
To lop our parent stems; and never more
Must vile, habitual cups of deadliness
Distort their noble natures, and unseat
The purpose of their souls. They must return
To ancient customs; live on game and maize;
Clothe them with skins, and love both wife and child,
Nor lift a hand in wrath against their race.
TECUMSEH. These are wise counsels which are noised afar,
And many nations have adopted them
And made them law.
PROPHET. These counsels were your own!
Good in themselves, they are too weak to sway
Our fickle race. I've much improved on them
Since the Great Spirit took me by the hand.
TECUMSEH. Improved! and how? Your mission was to lead
Our erring people back to ancient ways—
Too long o'ergrown—not bloody sacrifice.
They tell me that the prisoners you have ta'en—
Not captives in fair fight, but wanderers
Bewildered in our woods, or such as till

Outlying fields, caught from the peaceful plough—
You cruelly have tortured at the stake.
Nor this the worst! In order to augment
Your gloomy sway you craftily have played
Upon the zeal and frenzy of our tribes,
And, in my absence, hatched a monstrous charge
Of sorcery amongst them, which hath spared
Nor feeble age nor sex. Such horrid deeds
Recoil on us! Old Shataronra's grave
Sends up its ghost, and Tetaboxti's hairs—
White with sad years and counsel—singed by you!
In dreams and nightmares, float on every breeze.
Ambition's madness might stop short of this,
And shall if I have life.
PROPHET. The Great Spirit
Hath urged me, and still urges me to all.
He puts his hand to mine and leads me on.
Do you not hear him whisper even now—
"Thou art the Prophet?" All our followers
Behold in me a greater than yourself,
And worship me, and venture where I lead.
TECUMSEH. Your fancy is the common slip of fools,
Who count the lesser greater being near.
Dupe of your own imposture and designs,
I cannot bind your thoughts! but what you do
Henceforth must be my subject; so take heed,
And stand within my sanction lest you fall.
PROPHET. You are Tecumseh—else you should choke for this!
[Haughtily crosses the stage and pauses.]
Stay! Let me think! I must not break with him—
'Tis premature. I know his tender part,
And I shall touch it.
[Recrosses the stage.]
Brother, let me ask,
Do you remember how our father fell?
TECUMSEH. Who can forget Kanawha's bloody fray?
He died for home in battle with the whites.
PROPHET. And you remember, too, that boyish morn,
When all our braves were absent on the chase—
That morn when you and I half-dreaming lay
In summer grass, but woke to deadly pain
Of loud-blown bugles ringing through the air.
They came!—a rush of chargers from the woods,

With tramplings, cursings, shoutings manifold,
And headlong onset, fierce with brandished swords,
Of frontier troopers eager for the fight.
Scarce could a lynx have screened itself from sight,
So sudden the attack—yet, trembling there,
We crouched unseen, and saw our little town
Stormed, with vile slaughter of small babe and crone,
And palsied grandsire—you remember it?
TECUMSEH. Remember it! Alas, the echoing
Of that wild havoc lingers in my brain!
O wretched age, and injured motherhood,
And hapless maiden-wreck!
PROPHET. Yet this has been
Our endless history, and it is this
Which crams my very veins with cruelty.
My pulses bound to see those devils fall
Brained to the temples, and their women cast
As offal to the wolf.
TECUMSEH. Their crimes are great—
Our wrongs unspeakable! yet my revenge
Is open war. It never shall be said
Tecumseh's hate went armed with cruelty.
There's reason in revenge; but spare our own!
These gloomy sacrifices sap our strength;
And henceforth from your wizard scrutinies
I charge you to forbear. But who's the white
You hold as captive?
PROPHET. He is called LEFROY—
A captive, but too free to come and go.
Our warriors struck his trail by chance, and found
His tent close by the Wabash, where he lay
With sprained ankle, foodless and alone.
He had a book of pictures with him there
Of Long-Knife forts, encampments and their chiefs—
Most recognizable; so, reasoning thence,
Our warriors took him for a daring spy,
And brought him here, and tied him to the stake.
Then he declared he was a Saganash—
No Long-Knife he! but one who loved our race,
And would adopt our ways—with honeyed words,
Couched in sweet voice, and such appealing eyes
That Iena, our niece—who listened near—
Believing, rushed, and cut him from the tree.

I hate his smiles, soft ways, and smooth-paced tread,
And would, ere now, have killed him but for her;
For ever since, unmindful of her race,
She has upheld him, and our matrons think
That he has won her heart.
TECUMSEH. But not her hand! This cannot be, and I must see to it:
Red shall not marry white—such is our law.
But graver matters are upon the wing,
Which I must open to you. Know you, then,
The nation that has doomed our Council-Fires—
Splashed with our blood—will on its Father turn,
Once more, whose lion-paws, stretched o'er the sea,
Will sheathe their nails in its unnatural tides,
Till blood will flow, as free as pitch in spring,
To gum the chafed seams of our sinking bark.
This opportunity, well-nursed, will give
A respite to our wrongs, and heal our wounds;
And all our nations, knit by me and ranged
In headship with our Saganash allies,
Will turn the mortal issue 'gainst our foes,
And wall our threatened frontiers with their slain.
But till that ripened moment, not a sheaf
Of arrows should be wasted, not a brave
Should perish aimlessly, nor discord reign
Amongst our tribes, nor jealousy distrain
The large effects of valour. We must now
Pack all our energies. Our eyes and ears
No more must idle with the hour, but work
As carriers to the brain, where we shall store,
As in an arsenal, deep schemes of war!
[A noise and shouting without.]
But who is this?
[Enter BARRON accompanied and half-dragged by warriors. The PROPHET goes forward to meet him.]
BARRON. I crave protection as a messenger
And agent sent by General Harrison.
Your rude, unruly braves, against my wish,
Have dragged me here as if I were a spy.
PROPHET. What else!
Why come you here if not a spy?
Brouillette came, and Dubois, who were spies—
Now you are here. Look on it! There's your grave.

[Pointing to the ground at BARRON'S feet.]
TECUMSEH. (Joining them.) Unhand this man!
He is a messenger, And not a spy.
Your life, my friend, is safe
In these rough woods as in your general's town.
But, quick—your message?
BARRON. The Governor of Indiana sends
This letter to you, in the which he says (Reading letter)
"You are an enemy to the Seventeen Fires.
I have been told that you intend to lift
The hatchet 'gainst your father, the great Chief,
Whose goodness, being greater than his fear
Or anger at your folly, still would stretch
His bounty to his children who repent,
And ask of him forgiveness for the past.
Small harm is done which may not be repaired,
And friendship's broken chain may be renewed;
But this is in your doing, and depends
Upon the choice you make. Two roads
Are lying now before you: one is large,
Open and pleasant, leading unto peace,
Your own security and happiness;
The other—narrow, crooked and constrained—
Most surely leads to misery and death.
Be not deceived! All your united force
Is but as chaff before the Seventeen Fires.
Your warriors are brave, but so are ours;
Whilst ours are countless as the forest leaves,
Or grains of sand upon the Wabash shores.
Rely not on the English to protect you!
They are not able to protect themselves.
They will not war with us, for, if they do,
Ere many moons have passed our battle flag
Shall wave o'er all the forts of Canada.
What reason have you to complain of us?
What have we taken? or what treaties maimed?
You tell us we have robbed you of your lands—
Bought them from nameless braves and village chiefs
Who had no right to sell—prove that to us,
And they will be restored. I have full power
To treat with you. Bring your complaint to me,
And I, in honor, pledge your safe return."

TECUMSEH. Is this it all?
BARRON. Yes, all. I have commands
To bear your answer back without delay.
PROPHET. This is our answer, then, to Harrison:
Go tell that bearded liar we shall come,
With forces which will pledge our own return!
TECUMSEH. What shall my answer be?
PROPHET. Why, like my own—There is no answer save that we shall go.
TECUMSEH. (To BARRON.) I fear that our complaint
lies all too deep For your Chief's curing. The Great
Spirit gave
The red men this wide continent as theirs,
And in the east another to the white;
But, not content at home, these crossed the sea,
And drove our fathers from their ancient seats.
Their sons in turn are driven to the Lakes,
And cannot further go unless they drown.
Yet now you take upon yourselves to say
This tract is Kickapoo, this Delaware,
And this Miami; but your Chief should know
That all our lands are common to our race!
How can one nation sell the rights of all
Without consent of all? No! For my part I am a Red Man,
not a Shawanoe,
And here I mean to stay. Go to your chief,
And tell him I shall meet him at Vincennes.
[Exeunt all but TECUMSEH.]
What is there in my nature so supine
That I must ever quarrel with revenge?
From vales and rivers which were once our own
The pale hounds who uproot our ancient graves
Come whining for our lands, with fawning tongues,
And schemes and subterfuge and subtleties.
O for a Pontiac to drive them back
And whoop them to their shuddering villages!
O for an age of valour like to his,
When freedom clothed herself with solitude,
And one in heart the scattered nations stood,
And one in hand. It comes! and mine shall be
The lofty task to teach them to be free—
To knit the nations, bind them into one,
And end the task great Pontiac begun!

SCENE II.
ANOTHER PART OF THE FOREST.

Enter LEFROY, carrying his rifle, and examining a knot of wild flowers.
LEFROY. This region is as lavish of its flowers
As Heaven of its primrose blooms by night.
This is the Arum which within its root
Folds life and death; and this the Prince's Pine,
Fadeless as love and truth—the fairest form
That ever sun-shower washed with sudden rain.
This golden cradle is the Moccasin Flower,
Wherein the Indian hunter sees his hound;
And this dark chalice is the Pitcher-Plant
Stored with the water of forgetfulness.
Whoever drinks of it, whose heart is pure,
Will sleep for aye 'neath foodful asphodel,
And dream of endless love. I need it not!
I am awake, and yet I dream of love.
It is the hour of meeting, when the sun
Takes level glances at these mighty woods,
And Iena has never failed till now,
To meet me here! What keeps her? Can it be
The Prophet? Ah, that villain has a thought,
Undreamt of by his simple followers,
Dark in his soul as midnight! If—but no—
He fears her though he hates! What shall I do?
Rehearse to listening woods, or ask these oaks
What thoughts they have, what knowledge of the past?
They dwarf me with their greatness, but shall come
A meaner and a mightier than they,
And cut them down. Yet rather would I dwell
With them, with wildness and its stealthy forms—
Yea, rather with wild men, wild beasts and birds,
Than in the sordid town that here may rise.
For here I am a part of Nature's self,
And not divorced from her like men who plod
The weary streets of care in search of gain.
And here I feel the friendship of the earth:
Not the soft cloying tenderness of hand
Which fain would satiate the hungry soul
With household honey-combs and parloured sweets,
But the strong friendship of primeval things—
The rugged kindness of a giant heart,

And love that lasts. I have a poem made
Which doth concern earth's injured majesty—
Be audience, ye still untroubled stems!
(Recites)
There was a time on this fair continent
When all things throve in spacious peacefulness.
The prosperous forests unmolested stood,
For where the stalwart oak grew there it lived
Long ages, and then died among its kind.
The hoary pines—those ancients of the earth—
Brimful of legends of the early world,
Stood thick on their own mountains unsubdued.
And all things else illumined by the sun,
Inland or by the lifted wave, had rest.
The passionate or calm pageants of the skies
No artist drew; but in the auburn west
Innumerable faces of fair cloud
Vanished in silent darkness with the day.
The prairie realm—vast ocean's paraphrase—
Rich in wild grasses numberless, and flowers
Unnamed save in mute Nature's inventory
No civilized barbarian trenched for gain.
And all that flowed was sweet and uncorrupt.
The rivers and their tributary streams,
Undammed, wound on forever, and gave up
Their lonely torrents to weird gulfs of sea,
And ocean wastes unshadowed by a sail.
And all the wild life of this western world
Knew not the fear of man; yet in those woods,
And by those plenteous streams and mighty lakes,
And on stupendous steppes of peerless plain,
And in the rocky gloom of canyons deep,
Screened by the stony ribs of mountains hoar
Which steeped their snowy peaks in purging cloud,
And down the continent where tropic suns
Warmed to her very heart the mother earth,
And in the congeal'd north where silence self
Ached with intensity of stubborn frost,
There lived a soul more wild than barbarous;
A tameless soul—the sunburnt savage free—
Free, and untainted by the greed of gain:
Great Nature's man content with Nature's food.
But hark! I hear her footsteps in the leaves—

And so my poem ends.
Enter IENA, downcast.
My love! my love!
What! Iena in tears! your looks, like clouds,
O'erspread my joy which, but a moment past,
Rose like the sun to high meridian.
Ah, how is this? She trembles, and she starts,
And looks with wavering eyes through oozing tears,
As she would fly from me. Why do you weep?
IENA. I weep, for I have come to say—farewell.
LEFROY. Farewell! I have fared well in love till now;
For you are mine, and I am yours, so say
Farewell, farewell, a thousand times farewell.
IENA. How many meanings has the word? since yours
Is full of joy, but mine, alas, of pain.
The pale-face and the Shawanoe must part.
LEFROY. Must part? Yes part—we parted yesterday—
And shall to-day—some dream disturbs my love.
IENA. Oh, that realities were dreams! 'Tis not
A dream that parts us, but a stern command.
Tecumseh has proclaimed it as his law—
Red shall not marry white; so must you leave;
And therefore I have come to say farewell.
LEFROY. That word is barbed, and like an arrow aimed.
The maid who saved my life would mar it too!
IENA. Speak not of that! Your life's in danger now.
Tecumseh has returned, and—knowing all—
Has built a barrier betwixt our loves,
More rigid than a palisade of oak.
LEFROY. What means he? And what barrier is this?
IENA. The barrier is the welfare of our race—
Wherefore his law—"Red shall not marry white."
His noble nature halts at cruelty,
So fear him not! But in the Prophet's hand,
Dark, dangerous and bloody, there is death,
And, sheltered by Tecumseh's own decree,
He who misprizes you, and hates, will strike—
Then go at once! Alas for Iena,
Who loves her race too well to break its law.
LEFROY. I love you better than I love my race;
And could I mass my fondness for my friends,
Augment it with my love of noble brutes,
Tap every spring of reverence and respect,

And all affections bright and beautiful—
Still would my love for you outweigh them all.
IENA. Speak not of love! Speak of the Long-Knife's
hate!
Oh, it is pitiful to creep in fear
O'er lands where once our fathers stept in pride!
The Long-Knife strengthens, whilst our race decays,
And falls before him as our forests fall.
First comes his pioneer, the bee, and soon
The mast which plumped the wild deer fats his swine.
His cattle pasture where the bison fed;
His flowers, his very weeds, displace our own—
Aggressive as himself. All, all thrust back!
Destruction follows us, and swift decay.
Oh, I have lain for hours upon the grass,
And gazed into the tenderest blue of heaven—
Cleansed as with dew, so limpid, pure and sweet—
All flecked with silver packs of standing cloud
Most beautiful! But watch them narrowly!
Those clouds will sheer small fleeces from their sides,
Which, melting in our sight as in a dream,
Will vanish all like phantoms in the sky.
So melts our heedless race! Some weaned away,
And wedded to rough-handed pioneers,
Who, fierce as wolves in hatred of our kind,
Yet from their shrill and acid women turn,
Prizing our maidens for their gentleness.
Some by outlandish fevers die, and some—
Caught in the white man's toils and vices mean—
Court death, and find it in the trader's cup.
And all are driven from their heritage,
Far from our fathers' seats and sepulchres,
And girdled with the growing glooms of war;
Resting a moment here, a moment there,
Whilst ever through our plains and forest realms
Bursts the pale spoiler, armed, with eager quest,
And ruinous lust of land. I think of all—
And own Tecumseh right. 'Tis he alone
Can stem this tide of sorrows dark and deep;
So must I bend my feeble will to his,
And, for my people's welfare, banish love.
LEFROY. Nay, for your people's welfare keep your love!
My heart is true: I know that braggart nation,

Whose sordid instincts, cold and pitiless,
Would cut you off, and drown your Council-Fires.
I would defend you, therefore keep me here!
My love is yours alone, my hand I give,
With this good weapon in it, to your race.
IENA. Oh, heaven help a weak untutored maid,
Whose head is warring 'gainst a heart that tells,
With every throb, I love you. Leave me! Fly!
LEFROY. I kneel to you—it is my leave-taking,
So, bid me fly again, and break my heart!
(IENA sings.)
Fly far from me,
Even as the daylight flies,
And leave me in the darkness of my pain!
Some earlier love will come to thee again,
And sweet new moons will rise,
And smile on it and thee.
Fly far from me,
Even whilst the daylight wastes—
Ere thy lips burn me in a last caress;
Ere fancy quickens, and my longings press,
And my weak spirit hastes
For shelter unto thee!
Fly far from me,
Even whilst the daylight pales—
So shall we never, never meet again!
Fly! for my senses swim—Oh, Love! Oh, Pain!—
Help! for my spirit fails—
I cannot fly from thee!
[IENA sinks into LEFROY'S arms.]
LEFROY. No Iena! You cannot fly from me—
My heart is in your breast, and yours in mine;
Therefore our love—
Enter TECUMSEH, followed by MAMATEE.
TECUMSEH. False girl! Is this your promise?
Would that I had a pale-face for a niece—
Not one so faithless to her pledge! You owe
All duty and affection to your race,
Whose interest—the sum of our desires—
Traversed by alien love, drops to the ground.
IENA. Tecumseh ne'er was cruel until now.
Call not love alien which includes our race—
Love for our people, pity for their wrongs!

He loves our race because his heart is here—
And mine is in his breast. Oh, ask him there,
And he will tell you—
LEFROY. Iena, let me speak!
Tecumseh, we as strangers have become
Strangely familiar through sheer circumstance,
Which often breeds affection or disdain,
Yet lighting but the surface of the man,
Shows not his heart. I know not what you think,
And care not for your favour or your love,
Save as desert may crown me. Your decree,
"Red shall not marry white," is arbitrary,
And off the base of nature; for if they
Should marry not, then neither should they love.
Yet Iena loves me, and I love her.
Be merciful! I ask not Iena
To leave her race; I rather would engage
These willing arms in her defence and yours.
Heap obligation up, conditions stern—
But send not your cold "Nay" athwart our lives.
IENA. Be merciful! Oh, uncle, pity us!
TECUMSEH. My pity, Iena, goes with reproach,
Blunting the edge of anger; yet my will
Is fixed, and the command to be obeyed—
This stranger must depart—you to your lodge!
MAMATEE. Tecumseh, I am in the background here,
As ever I have been in your affection.
For I have ne'er known what good women prize—
Earth's greatest boon to them—a husband's love.
TECUMSEH. My nation has my love, in which you share,
With special service rendered to yourself;
So that your cabin flows with mouffles sweet,
And hips of wapiti and bedded robes.
Teach me my duty further if you will!
My love is wide, and broods upon my race.
MAMATEE. The back is clad—the heart, alas! goes bare.
Oh, I would rather shiver in the snow—
My heart downed softly with Tecumseh's love—
Than sleep unprized in warmest couch of fur.
I know your love is wide, and, for that I
Share but a millionth part of it, and feel
Its meagreness, I plead most eagerly
For this poor white, whose heart is full of love,

And gives it all to her.
TECUMSEH. It cannot be!
You know not what you ask. 'Tis 'gainst our law,
Which, breached, would let our untamed people through.
LEFROY. I care not for your cruel law! The heart
Has statutes of its own which make for love.
TECUMSEH. You'd cross me too! This child's play of the heart,
Which sterner duty has repressed in me,
Makes even captives bold. (Aside.) I like his courage!
MAMATEE. If duty makes Tecumseh's heart grow cold,
Then shame on it! and greater shame on him
Who ever yet showed mercy to his foes,
Yet, turning from his own, in pity's spite
Denies it to a girl. See, here I kneel!
IENA. And I! O uncle, frown not on our love!
TECUMSEH. By the Great Spirit this is over much!
My heart is made for pity, not for war,
Since women's tears unman me. Have your will!
I shall respect your love, (To Lefroy.) your safety too.
I go at once to sound the Wyandots
Concerning some false treaties with the whites.
The Prophet hates you, therefore come with me.
[The PROPHET rushes in with a band of Braves.]
PROPHET. She's here! Take hold of her and bear her off!
TECUMSEH. (Menacingly) Beware! Lay not a finger on the girl!
[The Braves fall back.]
PROPHET. There is no law Tecumseh will not break,
When women weep, and pale-face spies deceive.
MAMATEE. Ah, wretch! not all our people's groans could wring
A single tear from out your murderous eye.
PROPHET. This is my captive, and his life is mine!
[Seizing LEFROY, and lifting his hatchet.]
IENA. (Rushing to LEFROY) Save him! Save him!
TECUMSEH. Your life will go for his—
One blow and you are doomed!
[TECUMSEH grasps the PROPHET'S uplifted axe.]

END OF FIRST ACT

CHARLES MAIR

ACT II. TECUMSEH

SCENE FIRST:
BEFORE THE PROPHET'S TOWN.

Enter TECUMSEH and LEFROY.
TECUMSEH. No guard or outlook—here! This is most strange.
Chance reigns where prudence sleeps!
Enter a BRAVE.
Here comes a brave
With frenzy in his face
Where is the Prophet?
BRAVE. He fasts alone within the medicine-lodge,
And talks to our Great Spirit. All our braves,
Huddling in fear, stand motionless without,
Thrilled by strange sounds, and voices not of earth.
TECUMSEH. How long has it been thus?
BRAVE. Four nights have passed
And none have seen his face; but all have heard
His dreadful tongue, in incantations deep,
Fetch horrors up—vile beings flashed from hell,
Who fought as devils fight, until the lodge
Shook to its base with struggling, and the earth
Quaked as, with magic strength, he flung them down.
These strove with him for mastery of our fate;
But, being foiled, Yohewa has appeared,
And, in the darkness of our sacred lodge,
Communes with him.

TECUMSEH. Our Spirit great and good!
He comes not here for nought. What has he promised?
BRAVE. Much! for henceforth we are invulnerable.
The bullets of the Long-Knives will rebound,
Like petty hailstones, from our naked breasts;
And, in the misty morns of our attack,
Strange lights will shine on them to guide our aim,
Whilst clouds of gloom will screen us from their sight.
TECUMSEH. The Prophet is a wise interpreter,
And all his words, by valour backed, will stand;
For valour is the weapon of the soul,
More dreaded by our vaunting enemies
Than the plumed arrow, or the screaming ball.
What wizardry and witchcraft has he found
Conspiring 'gainst our people's good?
BRAVE. Why, none! Wizard and witch are weeded out, he says;
Not one is left to do us hurt.
TECUMSEH. 'Tis well! My brother has the eyeball of the horse,
And swerves from danger. (Aside.) Bid our
warriors come! I wait them here.
[Exit BRAVE.]
The Prophet soon will follow.
LEFROY. Now opportunity attend my heart
Which waits for Iena! True love's behest,
Outrunning war's, will bring her to my arms
Ere cease the braves from gasping wonderment.
TECUMSEH. First look on service ere you look on love;
You shall not see her here.
LEFROY. My promises
Are sureties of my service—
TECUMSEH. But your deeds,
Accomplishments; our people count on deeds.
Be patient! Look upon our warriors
Roped round with scars and cicatrized wounds,
Inflicted in deep trial of their spirit
Their skewered sides are proofs of manly souls,
Which—had one groan escaped from agony—
Would all have sunk beneath our women's heels,
Unfit for earth or heaven. So try your heart,
And let endurance swallow all love's sighs.
Yoke up your valour with our people's cause,

And I, who love your nation, which is just,
When deeds deserve it, will adopt you here,
By ancient custom of our race, and join Iena's hand to
yours.
LEFROY. Your own hand first In pledge of this!
TECUMSEH. It ever goes with truth!
LEFROY. Now come some wind of chance, and show me her
But for one heavenly moment! as when leaves
Are blown aside in summer, and we see
The nested oriole.
[Enter Chiefs and warriors—The warriors cluster around TECUMSEH, shouting and discharging their pieces.]
TECUMSEH. My chiefs and braves!
MIAMI CHIEF. Fall back! Fall back! Ye press too close on him.
TECUMSEH. My friends! our joy is like to meeting
streams,
Which draw into a deep and prouder bed.
[Shouts from the warriors.]
DELAWARE CHIEF. Silence, ye braves! let great Tecumseh speak!
[The warriors fall back.]
TECUMSEH. Comrades, and faithful warriors of our race!
Ye who defeated Hartnar and St Clair,
And made their hosts a winter's feast for wolves!
I call on you to follow me again,
Not now for war, but as forearmed for fight.
As ever in the past so is it still:
Our sacred treaties are infringed and torn;
Laughed out of sanctity, and spurned away;
Used by the Long-Knife's slave to light his fire,
Or turned to kites by thoughtless boys, whose wrists
Anchor their fathers' lies in front of heaven.
And now we're asked to Council at Vincennes;
To bend to lawless ravage of our lands,
To treacherous bargains, contracts false, wherein
One side is bound, the other loose as air!
Where are those villains of our race and blood
Who signed the treaties that unseat us here;
That rob us of rich plains and forests wide;
And which, consented to, will drive us hence
To stage our lodges in the Northern Lakes,
In penalties of hunger worse than death?
Where are they? that we may confront them now
With your wronged sires, your mothers, wives and babes,

And, wringing from their false and slavish lips
Confession of their baseness, brand with shame
The traitor hands which sign us to our graves.
MIAMI CHIEF. Some are age-bent and blind, and others sprawl,
And stagger in the Long-Knife's villages;
And some are dead, and some have fled away,
And some are lurking in the forest here,
Sneaking, like dogs, until resentment cools.
KICKAPOO CHIEF. We all disclaim their treaties. Should they come,
Forced from their lairs by hunger, to our doors,
Swift punishment will light upon their heads.
TECUMSEH. Put yokes upon them! let their mouths be bound!
For they are swine who root with champing jaws
Their fathers' fields, and swallow their own offspring.
Enter the PROPHET in his robe—his face discoloured.
The Prophet! Welcome, my brother, from the lodge of dreams!
Hail to thee, sagest among men—great heir
Of all the wisdom of Pengasega!
PROPHET. This pale-face here again! this hateful snake,
Who crawls between our people and their laws!
(Aside.)
Your greeting, brother, takes the chill from mine,
When last we parted you were not so kind.
TECUMSEH. The Prophet's wisdom covers all. He knows
Why Nature varies in her handiwork,
Moulding one man from snow, the next from fire—
PROPHET. Which temper is your own, and blazes up,
In winds of passion like a burning pine.
TECUMSEH. 'Twill blaze no more unless to scorch our foes.
My brother, there's my hand—for I am grieved
That aught befell to shake our proper love.
Our purpose is too high, and full of danger;
We have too vast a quarrel on our hands
To waste our breath on this.
[Steps forward and offers his hand.]
PROPHET. My hand to yours.
SEVERAL CHIEFS. Tecumseh and the Prophet are rejoined!
TECUMSEH. Now, but one petty cloud distains our sky.

My brother, this man loves our people well.
[Pointing to LEFROY.]
LEFROY. I know he hates me, yet I hope to win
My way into his heart.
PROPHET. There—take my hand! I must dissemble.
Would this palm were poison! (Aside.) (To
TECUMSEH)
What of the Wyandots? And yet I know!
I have been up among the clouds, and down
Into the entrails of the earth, and seen
The dwelling-place of devils. All my dreams
Are from above, and therefore favour us.
TECUMSEH. With one accord the Wyandots disclaim
The treaties of Fort Wayne, and burn with rage.
Their tryst is here, and some will go with me
To Council at Vincennes. Where's Winnemac?
MIAMI CHIEF. That recreant has joined our enemies,
And with the peace-pipe sits beside their fire,
And whins away our lives.
KICKAPOO CHIEF. The Deaf-Chief, too,
With head awry, who cannot hear us speak
Though thunder shouted for us from the skies,
Yet hears the Long-Knives whisper at Vincennes;
And, when they jest upon our miseries,
Grips his old leathern sides, and coughs with laughter.
DELAWARE CHIEF. And old Kanaukwa—famed when we were young—
Has hid his axe, and washed his honours off.
TECUMSEH. 'Tis honor he has parted with, not honors;
Good deeds are ne'er forespent, nor wiped away.
I know these men; they've lost their followers,
And, grasping at the shadow of command,
Where sway and custom once had realty,
By times, and turn about, follow each other.
They count for nought—but Winnemac is true,
Though over-politic; he will not leave us.
PROPHET. Those wizened snakes must be destroyed at once!
TECUMSEH. Have mercy, brother—those poor men are old.
PROPHET. Nay, I shall teaze them till they sting themselves;
Their rusty fangs are doubly dangerous.
TECUMSEH. What warriors are ready for Vincennes?
WARRIORS. All! All are ready. Tecumseh leads us on—we follow him.

TECUMSEH. Four hundred warriors will go with me,
All armed, yet only for security
Against the deep designs of Harrison.
For 'tis my purpose still to temporize,
Not break with him in war till once again
I scour the far emplacements of our tribes.
Then shall we close at once on all our foes.
They claim our lands, but we shall take their lives;
Drive out their thievish souls, and spread their bones
To bleach upon the misty Alleghanies;
Or make death's treaty with them on the spot,
And sign our bloody marks upon their crowns
For lack of schooling—ceding but enough
Of all the lands they covet for their graves.
MIAMI CHIEF. Tecumseh's tongue is housed in wisdom's cheeks;
His valour and his prudence march together.
DELAWARE CHIEF. 'Tis wise to draw the distant nations on.
This scheme will so extend the Long-Knife force,
In lines defensive stretching to the sea,
Their bands will be but morsels for our braves.
PROPHET. How long must this bold project take to ripen?
Time marches with the foe, and his surveyors
Already smudge our forests with their fires.
It frets my blood and makes my bowels turn
To see those devils blaze our ancient oaks,
Cry "right!" and drive their rascal pickets down.
Why not make war on them at once?
TECUMSEH. Not now! Time will make room for weightier affairs.
Be this the disposition for the hour:
Our warriors from Vincennes will all return,
Save twenty—the companions of my journey—
And this brave white, who longs to share our toil,
And win his love by deeds in our defence.
You, brother, shall remain to guard our town,
Our wives, our children, all that's dear to us—
Receive each fresh accession to our strength;
And from the hidden world, which you inspect,
Draw a divine instruction for their souls.
Go, now, ye noble chiefs and warriors!
Make preparation—I'll be with you soon.

To-morrow we shall make the Wabash boil,
And beat its current, racing to Vincennes.
[Exeunt all but TECUMSEH and the PROPHET.]
PROPHET. I shall return unto our sacred lodge,
And there invoke the Spirit of the Wind
To follow you, and blow good tidings back.
TECUMSEH. Our strait is such we need the help of heaven.
Use all your wisdom, brother, but—beware!
Pluck not our enterprise while it is green,
And breed no quarrel here till I return.
Avoid it as you would the rattling snake;
And, when you hear the sound of danger, shrink,
And face it not, unless with belts of peace.
White wampum, not the dark, till we can strike
With certain aim. Can I depend on you?
PROPHET. Trust you in fire to burn, or cold to freeze?
So may you trust in me. The heavy charge
Which you have laid upon my shoulders now
Would weigh the very soul of rashness down.
[Exit the PROPHET.]
TECUMSEH. I think I can depend on him—I must!
Yet do I know his crafty nature well—
His hatred of our foes, his love of self,
And wide ambition. What is mortal man?
Who can divine this creature that doth take
Some colour from all others? Nor shall I
Push cold conclusions 'gainst my brother's sum
Of what is good—so let dependence rest!
[Exit.]

SCENE SECOND
VINCENNES—A STREET.

Enter Citizens GERKIN, SLAUGH and TWANG.
GERKIN. Ain't it about time Barron was back, Jedge?
TWANG. I reckon so. Our Guvner takes a crazy sight more pains than I would to sweetin thet ragin' devil Tecumseh's temper. I'd sweetin it wi' sugar o lead ef I had my way.
SLAUGH. It's a reekin' shame—dang me ef it aint. End thet two-faced, one-eyed brother o' his, the Prophet.— I'll be darned ef folks don't say thet the Shakers in them 'ere parts claims him fer a disciple!
TWANG. Them Shakers is a queer lot. They dance jest like wild Injuns, and

thinks we orter be kind to the red rascals, end use them honestly.

GERKIN. Wall! Thet's what our Guvner ses tew. But I reckon he's shammin' a bit Twist you and me, he's on the make like the rest o' us. Think o' bein' kind to a red devil thet would lift your har ten minutes arter! End as fer honesty—I say "set 'em up" every time, and then rob 'em. Thet's the way to clar them out o' the kentry. Whiskey's better 'n gunpowder, end costs less than fightin' 'em in the long run.

Enter CITIZEN BLOAT.

TWANG. Thet's so! Hello, Major, what's up? You look kind o' riled to-day.

BLOAT. Wall, Jedge, I dew feel right mad—have you heerd the noos?

TWANG. No! has old Sledge bust you at the keerds again?

BLOAT. Old Sledge be darned! I had jest clar'd him out o' continentals—fifty to the shillin'—at his own game, when in ript Roudi—the Eyetalian that knifed the Muskoe Injun for peekin' through his bar-room winder last spring—jest down from Fort Knox. You know the chap, General; you was on his jury.

SLAUGH. I reckon I dew. The Court was agin him, but we acquitted him afore the Chief-Justice finished his charge, and gave him a vote o' thanks to boot. There's a heap o' furriners creepin' inter these parts—poor downtrodden cusses from Europe—end, ef they're all like Roudi, they'll dew—a'most as hendy wi' the knife as our own people. But what's up?

BLOAT. Roudi saw Barron at Fort Knox, restin' thar on his way back from the Prophet's Town, end he sez thet red assassin Tecumseh's a-cumin' down wi' four hundred o' his painted devils to convarse wi' our Guvner. They're all armed, he sez, end will be here afore mid-day.

SLAUGH. Wall! our Guvner notified him to come—he's only gettin' what he axed for. There'll be a deal o' loose har flitterin' about the streets afore night, I reckon. Harrison's a heap too soft wi' them red roosters; he h'aint got cheek enough.

GERKIN. I've heerd say the Guvner, end the Chief Justice tew, thinks a sight o' this tearin' red devil. They say he's a great man. They say, tew, thet our treaty Injuns air badly used—thet they shouldn't be meddled wi' on their resarves, end should hev skoolin'.

BLOAT. Skoolin'! That gits me! Dogoned ef I wouldn't larn them jest one thing—what them regler officers up to the Fort larns their dogs—"to drap to shot," only in a different kind o' way like; end, es fer their resarves, I say, give our farmers a chance—let them locate!

TWANG. Thet's so, Major! What arthly use air they— plouterin' about their little bits o' fields, wi' their little bits o' cabins, end livin' half the time on mush- rats? I say, let them move out, end give reliable citizens a chance.

SLAUGH. Wall, I reckon our Guvner's kind's about played out. They call themselves the old stock—the clean pea —the rale gentlemen o' the Revolooshun. But, gentlemen, ain't we the Revolooshun? Jest wait till the live citizens o' these United States end Territories gits a chance, end we'll show them gentry what a free people, wi' our institooshuns, kin do. There'll be no more talk o' skoolin fer Injuns, you bet! I'd give them Kernel Crunch's billet.

GERKIN. What was thet, General?

SLAUGH. Why, they say he killed a hull family o' redskins, and stuck 'em up as scar' crows in his wheat fields. Gentlemen, there's nothin' like original idees!

TWANG. Thet war an original idee! The Kernel orter hev tuk out a patent. I think I've heerd o' Crunch. Wam't he wi' Kernel Crawford, o' the melish', at one time?

SLAUGH Whar?

TWANG. Why over to the Muskingum. You've heerd o' them Delaware Moravians over to the Muskingum, surely?

SLAUGH. Oh, them convarted chaps! but I a'most forgit the carcumstance.

TWANG. Wall, them red devils had a nice resarve thar— as yieldin' a bit o' sile as one could strike this side o' the Alleghanies. They was all convarted by the Moravians, end pertended to be as quiet and peaceable as the Shakers hereabout But Kernel Crawford—who knew good sile when he sot his eyes on it—diskivered thet them prayin' chaps had helped a war-party from the North, wi' provisions—or thort they did, which was the same thing. So—one fine Sunday—he surrounds their church wi' his melish'—when the Injuns was all a- prayin'—end walks in himself, jest for a minute or two, end prays a bit so as not to skeer them tew soon, end then walks out, end locks the door. The Kernel then cutely—my heart kind o' warms to thet man—put a squad o' melish' at each winder wi' their bayonets pinted, end sot fire to the Church, end charred up the hull kit, preacher and all! The heft o' them was burnt; but some thet warn't thar skinned out o' the kentry, end got lands from the British up to the Thames River in Canady, end founded what they call the Moravian Towns thar; and thar they is still—fur them Britishers kind o' pampers the Injuns, so they may git at our scalps.

SLAUGH. I reckon we'll hev a tussle wi' them gentry afore long. But for Noo England we'd a hed it afore now; but them Noo Englanders kind o' curries to the Britishers. A war would spile their shippin', end so they're agin it. But we h'aint got no ships to spile in this western kentry, end so I reckon we'll pitch in.

GERKIN. We'd better git out o' this Injun fry-pan fust, old hoss! I could lick my own weight in wild-cats, but this ruck o' Injuns is jest a little tew hefty.

BLOAT. Maybe they want to come to skool, end start store, end sich!

GERKIN. Gentlemen—I mean to send my lady down stream, end I reckon you'd better dew the same wi' your 'uns— jest fer safety like. My time's

limited—will you liquor?
ALL. You bet!
BLOAT. (Meditatively) Skoolin! Wall, I'll be darned!
[Exeunt.]

SCENE THIRD.
THE SAME. A ROOM IN GENERAL HARRISON'S HOUSE.

Enter GENERAL HARRISON, and some Officers of the American Army.
HARRISON. What savage handiwork keeps Barron back?
Enter BARRON.
Ah, here he comes, his looks interpreting Mischief and failure! It is as I feared. What answer do you bring?
BARRON. Tecumseh comes
To council, with four hundred men at back,
To which, with all persuasion, I objected—
As that it would alarm our citizens,
Whose hasty temper, by suspicion edged,
Might break in broils of quarrel with his braves;
But, sir, it was in vain—so be prepared!
Your Council records may be writ in blood.
HARRISON. Will he attack us, think you?
BARRON. No, not now. His present thought is to intimidate.
But, lest some rash and foulmouthed citizen
Should spur his passion to the run, fore-arm!
HARRISON. Tut! Arms are scarce as soldiers in our town,
And I am sick of requisitioning.
Nay, we must trust to something else than arms.
Tecumseh is a savage but in name—Let's trust to him!
What says he of our treaties?
BARRON. O, he discharges them as heavy loads,
Which borne by red men only, break their backs.
All lands, he says, are common to his race;
Not to be sold but by consent of all.
HARRISON. Absurd! This proposition would prevent
All purchase and all progress. No, indeed;
We cannot tie our hands with such conditions.
What of the Prophet? Comes he with the rest?
BARRON. The Prophet stays behind.
HARRISON. He is a foil
Used by Tecumseh to augment his greatness;
And, by good husbandry of incantation,

And gloomy charms by night, this Prophet works
So shrewdly on their braves that every man,
Inflamed by auguries of victory,
Would rush on death.
1ST OFFICER. Why, General, I heard He over-trumpt you once and won the trick.
HARRISON. How so?
1ST OFFICER. Well, once, before his braves, 'tis said,
You dared him to a trial of his spells,
Which challenge he accepted, having heard
From white men of a coming sun-eclipse.
Then, shrewdly noting day and hour, he called
Boldly his followers round him, and declared
That he would hide the sun. They stood and gazed,
And, when the moon's colossal shadow fell,
They crouched upon the ground, and worshipped him.
HARRISON. He caught me there, and mischief came of it.
Oh, he is deep. How different those brothers!
One dipt in craft, the dye of cruelty,
The other frank and open as the day.
Enter an ORDERLY.
ORDERLY. Tecumseh and his braves have reached the landing!
[Excitement. All rise hastily.]
HARRISON. This room is smaller than our audience:
Take seats and benches to the portico—
There we shall treat with him.
[Exeunt all but GENERAL HARRISON.]
Could I but strain
My charge this chief might be our trusty friend.
Yet I am but my nation's servitor;
Gold is the king who overrides the right,
And turns our people from the simple ways,
And fair ideal of our fathers' lives.
[Exit.]

SCENE FOURTH.
THE SAME. THE PORTICO OF GENERAL HARRISON'S HOUSE.
AN OPEN GROVE AT A LITTLE DISTANCE IN FRONT.

[Curtain rises and discovers GENERAL HARRISON, army officers and citizens, of various quality, including TWANG, SLAUGH, GERKIN and BLOAT, _seated in the portico. A sergeant and guard of soldiers near by. Enter_ TECUMSEH and his followers with LEFROY in Indian dress.

They all stop at the grove.]
HARRISON. Why halts he there? Go tell him he is welcome to our house.
[An Orderly goes down with message.]
1ST OFFICER. How grave and decorous they look— "the mien Of pensive people born in ancient woods." But look at him! Look at Tecumseh there— How simple in attire! that eagle, plume Sole ornament, and emblem of his spirit. And yet, far-scanned, there's something in his face That likes us not. Would we were out of this!
HARRISON. Yes; even at a distance I can see
His eyes distilling anger. 'Tis no sign
Of treachery, which ever drapes with smiles
The most perfidious purpose. Our poor strength
Would fall at once should he break out on us;
But let us hope 'tis yet a war of wits
Where firmness may enact the part of force.
[Orderly returns.]
What answer do you bring?
ORDERLY. Tecumseh says: "Houses are built for whites— the red man's house, Leaf-roofed, and walled with living oak, is there—
[Pointing to the grove.]
Let our white brother meet us in it!"
2ND OFFICER. Oh! White brother! So he levels to your height, And strips your office of its dignity.
3RD OFFICER. 'Tis plain he cares not for your dignity,
And touchingly reminds us of our tenets.
Our nation spurns the outward shows of state,
And ceremony dies for lack of service.
Pomp is discrowned, and throned regality
Dissolved away in our new land and laws.
Man is the Presence here!
1ST OFFICER. Well, for my part, I like not that one in particular.
[Pointing toward TECUMSEH.]
3RD OFFICER. No more do I! I wish I were a crab, And had its courtly fashion of advancing.
HARRISON. Best yield to him, the rather that he now
Invites our confidence. His heavy force
Scants good opinion somewhat, yet I know
There's honor, aye, and kindness in this Chief.
[Rising.]
3RD OFFICER. Yes, faith, he loves us all, and means to keep Locks of our hair for memory. Here goes.
[All rise.] Servants and soldiers carry chairs and benches to the grove, followed by GENERAL HARRISON _and others, who seat themselves—

_TECUMSEH and his followers still standing in the lower part of the grove.

HARRISON. We have not met to bury our respect, Or mar our plea with lack of courtesy. The Great Chief knows it is his father's wish That he should sit by him.

TECUMSEH. My father's wish! My father is the sun; the earth my mother [Pointing to each in turn.]
And on her mighty bosom I shall rest.
[TECUMSEH and his followers seat themselves on the grass.]

HARRISON. (Rising.) I asked Tecumseh to confer
with me,
Not in war's hue, but for the ends of peace.
Our own intent—witness our presence here,
Unarmed save those few muskets and our swords.
How comes it, then, that he descends on us
With this o'erbearing and untimely strength?
Tecumseh's virtues are the theme of all;
Wisdom and courage, frankness and good faith—
To speak of these things is to think of him!
Yet, as one theft makes men suspect the thief—
Be all his life else spent in honesty—
So does one breach of faithfulness in man
Wound all his after deeds. There is a pause
In some men's goodness like the barren time
Of those sweet trees which yield each second year,
Wherein what seems a niggardness in nature;
Is but good husbandry for future gifts.
But this tree bears, and bears most treacherous fruit!
Here is a gross infringement of all laws
That shelter men in council, where should sit
No disproportioned force save that of reason—
Our strong dependence still, and argument,
Of better consequence than that of arms,
If great Tecumseh should give ear to it.

TECUMSEH. (Rising.) You called upon Tecumseh and
he came!
You sent your messenger, asked us to bring
Our wide complaint to you—and it is here!
[Waving his arm toward his followers.]
Why is our brother angry at our force,
Since every man but represents a wrong?
Nay! rather should our force be multiplied!
Fill up your streets and overflow your fields,

And crowd upon the earth for standing room;
Still would our wrongs outweigh our witnesses,
And scant recital for the lack of tongues.
I know your reason, and its bitter heart,
Its form of justice, clad with promises—
The cloaks of death! That reason was the snare
Which tripped our ancestors in days of yore—
Who knew not falsehood and so feared it not:
Men who mistook your fathers' vows for truth,
And took them, cold and hungry, to their hearts.
Filled them with food, and shared with them their homes,
With such return as might make baseness blush.
What tree e'er bore such treacherous fruit as this?
But let it pass! let wrongs die with the wronged!
The red man's memory is full of graves.
But wrongs live with the living, who are here—
Inheritors of all our fathers' sighs,
And tears, and garments wringing wet with blood.
The injuries which you have done to us
Cry out for remedy, or wide revenge.
Restore the forests you have robbed us of—
Our stolen homes and vales of plenteous corn!
Give back the boundaries, which are our lives,
Ere the axe rise! aught else is reasonless.
HARRISON. Tecumseh's passion is a dangerous flood
Which sweeps away his judgment. Let him lift
His threatened axe to hit defenceless heads!
It cannot mar the body of our right,
Nor graze the even justice of our claim:
These still would live, uncancelled by our death.
Let reason rule us, in whose sober light
We read those treaties which offend him thus:
What nation was the first established here,
Settled for centuries, with title sound?
You know that people, the Miamies, well.
Long ere the white man tripped his anchors cold,
To cast them by the glowing western isles,
They lived upon these lands in peace, and none
Dared cavil at their claim. We bought from them,
For such equivalent to largess joined,
That every man was hampered with our goods,
And stumbled on profusion. But give ear!

Jealous lest aught might fail of honesty—
Lest one lean interest or poor shade of right
Should point at us—we made the Kickapoo
And Delaware the sharer of our gifts,
And stretched the arms of bounty over heads
Which held but by Miami sufferance.
But, you! whence came you? and what rights have you?
The Shawanoes are interlopers here—
Witness their name! mere wanderers from the South!
Spurned thence by angry Creek and Yamasee—
Now here to stir up strife, and tempt the tribes
To break the seals of faith. I am surprised
That they should be so led, and more than grieved
Tecumseh has such ingrates at his back.
TECUMSEH. Call you those ingrates who but claim their own,
And owe you nothing but revenge? Those men
Are here to answer and confront your lies.
[Turning to his followers.]
Miami, Delaware and Kickapoo!
Ye are alleged as signers of those deeds—
Those dark and treble treacheries of Fort Wayne.—
Ye chiefs whose cheeks are tanned with battle-smoke,
Stand forward then, and answer if you did it!
KICKAPOO CHIEF. (Rising.) Not I! I disavow them!
They were made By village chiefs whose vanity o'ercame
Their judgment, and their duty to our race.
DELAWARE CHIEF. (Rising.) And I reject the treaties in the name
Of all our noted braves and warriors.
They have no weight save with the palsied heads
Which dote on friendly compacts in the past.
MIAMI CHIEF. (Rising.) And I renounce them also.
They were signed By sottish braves—the Long-Knife's tavern-chiefs—
Who sell their honor like a pack of fur,
Make favour with the pale-face for his fee,
And caper with the hatchet for his sport.
I am a chief by right of blood, and fling
Your false and flimsy treaties in your face.
I am my nation's head, and own but one
As greater than myself, and he is here!
[Pointing to TECUMSEH.]

TECUMSEH. You have your answer, and from those whose rights
Stand in your own admission. But from me—
The Shawanoe—the interloper here—
Take the full draught of meaning, and wash down
Their dry and bitter truths. Yes! from the South
My people came—fall'n from their wide estate
Where Altamaha's uncongealing springs
Kept a perpetual summer in their sight—
Sweet with magnolia blooms, and dropping balm,
And scented breath of orange and of pine.
And from the East the hunted Delawares came,
Flushed from their coverts and their native streams;
Your old allies, men ever true to you,
Who, resting after long and weary flight,
Are by your bands shot sitting on the ground.
HARRISON. Those men got ample payment for their lands,
Full recompense, and just equivalent.
TECUMSEH. They flew from death to light upon it here!
And many a tribe comes pouring from the East,
Smitten with fire—their outraged women, maimed,
Screaming in horror o'er their murdered babes,
Whose sinless souls, slashed out by white men's swords,
Whimper in Heaven for revenge. Oh, God!—
'Tis thus the pale-face prays, then cries 'Amen':—
He clamours, and his Maker answers him,
Whilst our Great Spirit sleeps! O, no, no, no,—
He does not sleep! He will avenge our wrongs!
That Christ the white men murdered, and thought dead—
Who, if He died for mankind, died for us—
He is alive, and looks from heaven on this!
Oh, we have seen your baseness and your guile;
Our eyes are opened and we know your ways!
No longer shall you hoax us with your pleas,
Or with the serpent's cunning wake distrust,
Range tribe 'gainst tribe—then shoot the remnant down,
And in the red man's empty cabin grin,
And shake with laughter o'er his desolate hearth.
No, we are one! the red men all are one
In colour as in love, in lands and fate!
HARRISON. Still, with the voice of wrath Tecumseh speaks,
And not with reason's tongue.

TECUMSEH. O keep your reason! It is a thief which
steals away our lands.
Your reason is our deadly foe, and writes
The jeering epitaphs for our poor graves.
It is the lying maker of your books,
Wherein our people's vengeance is set down,
But not a word of crimes which led to it.
These are hushed up and hid, whilst all our deeds,
Even in self-defence, are marked as wrongs
Heaped on your blameless heads.
But to the point! Just as our brother's Seventeen
Council Fires
Unite for self-protection so do we.
How can you blame us, since your own example
Is but our model and fair precedent?
The Long-Knife's craft has kept our tribes apart,
Nourished dissensions, raised distinctions up,
Forced us to injuries which, soon as done,
Are made your vile pretexts for bloody war.
But this is past our nations now are one—
Ready to rise in their imbanded strength.
You promised to restore our ravaged lands
On proof that they are ours—that proof is here,
And by the tongues of truth has answered you.
Redeem your sacred pledges, and no more
Our "leaden birds" will sing amongst your corn:
But love will shine on you, and startled peace
Will come again, and build by every hearth.
Refuse—and we shall strike you to the ground!
Pour flame and slaughter on your confines wide,
Till the charred earth, up to the cope of Heaven,
Reeks with the smoke of smouldering villages,
And steam of awful fires half-quenched with blood.
[Citizens converse in undertones.]
TWANG. Did you ever hear the like! Ef I hed my shootin'- iron darn me ef I wouldn't draw a bead on thet barkin' savage. The hungry devil gits under-holts on our Guvner every time.
SLAUGH. You bet! I reckon he'd better put a lump o' bacon in his mouth to keep his bilin' sap o' passion down.
BLOAT. Thet's mor'n I'd do. This is jest what we git for allowin' the skulkin' devils to live. I'd vittle 'em on lead pills ef I was Guvner.
TWANG. Thet's so! Our civilizashun is jest this—we know what's what. Ef I hed my way—

HARRISON. Silence, you fools! If you provoke him here your blood be on your heads.
GERKIN. Right you air, Guvner! We'll close our dampers.
TECUMSEH. My brother's ears have heard. Where is his tongue?
HARRISON. My honest ears ache in default of reason.
Tecumseh is reputed wise, yet now
His fuming passions from his judgment fly,
Like roving steeds which gallop from the catch,
And kick the air, wasting in wantonness
More strength than in submission. His threats fall
On fearless ears. Knows he not of our force,
Which in the East swarms like mosquitoes here?
Our great Kentucky and Virginia fires?
Our mounted men and soldier-citizens?
These all have stings—let him beware of them!
TECUMSEH. Who does not know your vaunting citizens!
Well drilled in fraud and disciplined in crime;
But in aught else—as honor, justice, truth—
A rabble, and a base disordered herd.
We know them; and our nations, knit in one,
Will challenge them, should this, our last appeal,
Fall on unheeding ears. My brother, hearken!
East of Ohio you possess our lands,
Thrice greater than your needs, but west of it
We claim them all; then, let us make its flood
A common frontier, and a sacred stream
Of which our nations both may drink in peace.
HARRISON. Absurd! The treaties of Fort Wayne must stand.
Your village chiefs are heads of civil rule,
Whose powers you seek to centre in yourself,
Or vest in warriors whose trade is blood.
We bought from those, and from your peaceful men—
Your wiser brothers—who had faith in us.
TECUMSEH. Poor, ruined brothers, weaned from honest lives!
HARRISON. They knew our wisdom, and preferred to sell
Their cabins, fields, and wilds of unused lands
For rich reserves and ripe annuities.
As for your nations being one like ours—
'Tis false—else would they speak one common tongue.
Nay, more! your own traditions trace you here—
Widespread in lapse of ages through the land—
From o'er the mighty ocean of the West.

What better title have you than ourselves,
Who came from o'er the ocean of the East,
And meet with you on free and common ground?
Be reasonable, and let wisdom's words
Displace your passion, and give judgment vent
Think more of bounty, and talk less of rights—
Our hands are full of gifts, our hearts of love.
TECUMSEH. My brother's love is like the trader's warmth—
O'er with the purchase. Oh, unhappy lives—
Our gifts which go for yours! Once we were strong.
Once all this mighty continent was ours,
And the Great Spirit made it for our use.
He knew no boundaries, so had we peace
In the vast shelter of His handiwork,
And, happy here, we cared not whence we came.
We brought no evils thence—no treasured hate,
No greed of gold, no quarrels over God;
And so our broils, to narrow issues joined,
Were soon composed, and touched the ground of peace.
Our very ailments, rising from the earth,
And not from any foul abuse in us,
Drew back, and let age ripen to death's hand.
Thus flowed our lives until your people came,
Till from the East our matchless misery came!
Since then our tale is crowded with your crimes,
With broken faith, with plunder of reserves—
The sacred remnants of our wide domain—
With tamp'rings, and delirious feasts of fire,
The fruit of your thrice-cursed stills of death,
Which make our good men bad, our bad men worse,
Aye! blind them till they grope in open day,
And stumble into miserable graves.
Oh, it is piteous, for none will hear!
There is no hand to help, no heart to feel,
No tongue to plead for us in all your land.
But every hand aims death, and every heart,
Ulcered with hate, resents our presence here;
And every tongue cries for our children's land
To expiate their crime of being born.
Oh, we have ever yielded in the past,
But we shall yield no more! Those plains are ours!
Those forests are our birth-right and our home!

Let not the Long-Knife build one cabin there—
Or fire from it will spread to every roof,
To compass you, and light your souls to death!
HARRISON. Dreams he of closing up our empty plains?
Our mighty forests waiting for the axe?
Our mountain steeps engrailed with iron and gold?
There's no asylumed madness like to this!
Mankind shall have its wide possession here;
And these rough assets of a virgin world
Stand for its coming, and await its hand.
The poor of every land shall come to this,
Heart-full of sorrows and shall lay them down.
LEFROY. (Springing to his feet.) The poor!
What care your rich thieves for the poor?
Those graspers hate the poor, from whom they spring,
More deeply than they hate this injured race.
Much have they taken from it—let them now
Take this prediction, with the red man's curse!
The time will come when that dread power—the Poor—
Whom, in their greed and pride of wealth, they spurn—
Will rise on them, and tear them from their seats;
Drag all their vulgar splendours down, and pluck
Their shallow women from their lawless beds,
Yea, seize their puling and unhealthy babes,
And fling them as foul pavement to the streets.
In all the dreaming of the Universe
There is no darker vision of despairs!
1ST OFFICER. What man is that? 'Tis not an Indian.
HARRISON. Madman, you rave!—you know not what you say.
TECUMSEH. Master of guile, this axe should speak for him!
[Drawing his hatchet as if to hurl it at HARRISON.]
2ND OFFICER. This man means mischief! Quick! Bring up the guard!
[GENERAL HARRISON and officers draw their swords. The warriors spring to their feet and cluster about TECUMSEH, their eyes fixed intently upon HARRISON, who stands unmoved. TWANG and his friends disappear. The soldiers rush forward and take aim, but are ordered not to fire.]

END OF SECOND ACT

ACT III. TECUMSEH

SCENE FIRST.
VINCENNES.—A COUNCIL CHAMBER IN GENERAL HARRISON'S HOUSE.

Enter HARRISON and five COUNCILLORS.
HARRISON. Here are despatches from the President,
As well as letters from my trusted friends,
Whose tenor made me summon you to Council.
[Placing papers on table.]
1ST COUNCILLOR. Why break good news so gently? Is it true War is declared 'gainst England?
HARRISON. Would it were! That war is still deferred.
Our news is draff, And void of spirit, since New
England turns
A fresh cheek to the slap of Britain's palm.
Great God! I am amazed at such supineness.
Our trade prohibited, our men impressed,
Our flag insulted—still her people bend,
Amidst the ticking of their wooden clocks,
Bemused o'er small inventions. Out upon't!
Such tame submission yokes not with my spirit,
And sends my southern blood into my cheeks,
As proxy for New England's sense of shame.
2ND COUNCILLOR. We all see, save New England, what to do;
But she has eyes for her one interest—
A war might sink it. So the way to war

Puzzles imagining.
HARRISON. There is a way
Which lies athwart the President's command.
The reinforcements asked for from Monroe
Are here at last, but with this strict injunction,
They must not be employed save in defence,
Or in a forced attack.
[Taking up a letter.]
Now, here is news, Fresh from the South, of bold Tecumseh's work,
The Creeks and Seminoles have conjoined,
Which means a general union of the tribes,
And ravage of our Southern settlements.
Tecumseh's master hand is seen in this,
And these fresh tidings tally with his threats
Before he left Vincennes.
3RD COUNCILLOR. You had a close Encounter with him here.
HARRISON. Not over close, Nor dangerous—I saw he would not strike.
His thoughts outran his threats, and looked beyond
To wider fields and trials of our strength.
4TH COUNCILLOR. Our tree is now too bulky for his axe.
HARRISON. Don't underrate his power! But for our States
This man would found an empire to surpass
Old Mexico's renown, or rich Peru.
Allied with England, he is to be feared
More than all other men.
1ST COUNCILLOR. You had some talk In private, ere he vanished to the South?
HARRISON. Mere words, yet ominous. Could we restore
Our purchases, and make a treaty line,
All might be well; but who would stand to it?
2ND COUNCILLOR. It is not to be thought of.
OTHER COUNCILLORS. No, no, no.
HARRISON. In further parley at the river's edge,
Scenting a coming war, he clapped his hands,
And said the English whooped his people on,
As if his braves were hounds to spring at us;
Compared our nation to a whelming flood,
And called his scheme a dam to keep it back—
Then proffered the old terms; whereat I urged
A peaceful mission to the President.
But, by apt questions, gleaning my opinion,

Ere I was ware, of such a bootless trip,
He drew his manly figure up, then smiled,
And said our President might drink his wine
In safety in his distant town, whilst we—
Over the mountains here—should fight it out:
Then entering his bark, well-manned with braves,
Bade me let matters rest till he returned
From his far mission to the distant tribes,
Waved an adieu, and, in a trice, was gone.
2ND COUNCILLOR. Your news is but an earnest of his work.
4TH COUNCILLOR. This Chief's dispatch should be our own example.
Let matters rest, forsooth, till he can set
Our frontier in a blaze! Such cheap advice
Pulls with the President's, not mine.
HARRISON. Nor mine! The sum of my advice is to attack
The Prophet ere Tecumseh can return.
5TH COUNCILLOR. But what about the breach of your instructions?
HARRISON. If we succeed we need not fear the breach—
In the same space we give and heal the wound.
[Enter a Messenger, who hands letters to HARRISON.]
Thank you, Missouri and good Illinois—
Your governors are built of western clay.
Howard and Edwards both incline with me,
And urge attack upon the Prophet's force.
This is the nucleus of Tecumseh's strength—
His bold scheme's very heart. Let's cut it out.
Yes! yes! and every other part will fail.
1ST COUNCILLOR. Let us prepare to go at once!
2ND COUNCILLOR. Agreed.
3RD COUNCILLOR. I vote for war.
5TH COUNCILLOR. But should the Prophet win?
4TH COUNCILLOR. Why then, the Prophet, not Tecumseh, kills us—
Which has the keener axe?
1ST COUNCILLOR. Breech-clouted dogs! Let us attack them, and, with thongs of fire, Whip their red bodies to a deeper red.
HARRISON. This feeling bodes success, and with success
Comes war with England; for a well-won fight
Will rouse a martial spirit in the land
To emulate our deeds on higher ground.
Now hasten to your duties and prepare:
Bronzed autumn comes, when copper-colored oaks
Drop miserly their stiff leaves to the earth;

And ere the winter's snow doth silver them,
Our triumph must be wrought.
[Exeunt.]

SCENE SECOND.
TECUMSEH'S CABIN IN THE PROPHET'S TOWN.

[Enter IENA and MAMATEE, agitated.]
IENA. My heart is sad, and I am faint with fear.
My friend, my more than mother, go again—
Plead with the Prophet for a single day!
Perchance within his gloomy heart will stir
Some sudden pulse of pity for a girl.
MAMATEE. Alas, my Iena, it is in vain!
He swore by Manitou this very morn,
That thou should'st wed the chief, Tarhay, to-night.
IENA. Nay try once more, Oh Mamatee, once more!
I had a dream, and heard the gusty breeze
Hurtle from out a sea of hissing pines,
Then dwindle into voices, faint and sweet,
Which cried—we come! It was my love and yours!
They spoke to me—I know that they are near,
And waft their love to us upon the wind.
MAMATEE. Some dreams are merely fancies in our sleep:
I'll make another trial, but I feel
Your only safety is in instant flight.
IENA. Flight! Where and how—beset by enemies?
My fear sits like the partridge in the tree,
And cannot fly whilst these dogs bark at me.

SCENE THIRD.
AN ELEVATED PLATEAU, DOTTED WITH HEAVY OAKS, WEST OF THE PROPHET'S TOWN.

Enter three of HARRISON'S staff Officers.
1ST OFFICER. Well, here's the end of all our northward marching!
2ND OFFICER. A peaceful end, if we can trust those chiefs Who parleyed with us lately.
3RD OFFICER. Yes, for if They mean to fight, why point us to a spot At once so strong and pleasant for our camp?
1ST OFFICER. Report it so unto our General!
[Exit 3RD OFFICER.]
'Tis worth our long march through the forest wild

To view these silent plains! The Prophet's Town,
Sequestered yonder like a hermitage,
Disturbs not either's vast of solitude,
But rather gives, like graveyard visitors,
To deepest loneliness a deeper awe.
[Re enter 3RD OFFICER.]
3RD OFFICER. I need not go, for Harrison is here.
[Enter GENERAL HARRISON, his force following.]
1ST OFFICER. Methinks you like the place; some thanks we owe Unto the Prophet's chiefs for good advice.
HARRISON. (Looking around keenly).
These noble oaks, the streamlet to our rear,
This rank wild grass—wood, water and soft beds!
The soldier's luxuries are here together.
1ST OFFICER. Note, too, the place o'erlooks the springy plain
Which lies betwixt us and the Prophet's Town.
I think, sir, 'tis a very fitting place.
HARRISON. A fitting place if white men were our foes;
But to the red it gives a clear advantage.
Sleep like the weasel here, if you are wise!
1ST OFFICER. Why, sir, their chiefs, so menacing at first,
Became quite friendly at the last. They fear
A battle, and will treat on any terms.
The Prophet's tide of strength will ebb away,
And leave his stranded bark upon the mire.
HARRISON. 'Tis the mixed craft of old dissembling Nature!
If I could look upon her smallest web,
And see in it but crossed and harmless hairs,
Then might I trust the Prophet's knotted seine.
I did not like the manner of those chiefs
Who spoke so fairly. What but highest greatness
Plucks hatred from its seat, and in its stead
Plants friendship in an instant? This our camp
Is badly placed; each coulee and ravine
Is dangerous cover for approach by night;
And all the circuit of the spongy plain
A treacherous bog to mire our cavalry.
They who directed us so warmly here
Had other than our comfort in their eye.
2ND OFFICER. Fear you a night-attack, sir?

HARRISON. Fear it! No! I but anticipate, and shall
prepare.
'Tis sunset, and too late for better choice,
Else were the Prophet welcome to his ground.
Pitch tents and draw our baggage to the centre;
Girdle the camp with lynx-eyed sentinels;
Detail strong guards of choice and wakeful men
As pickets in advance of all oar lines;
Place mounted riflemen on both our flanks;
Our cavalry take post in front and rear,
But still within the lines of infantry,
Which, struck at any point, must hold the ground
Until relieved. Cover your rifle pans—
The thick clouds threaten rain. I look to you
To fill these simple orders to the letter.
But stay! Let all our camp fires burn
Till, if attacked, we form—then drown them out.
The darkness falls—make disposition straight;
Then, all who can, to sleep upon their arms.
I fear me, ere night yields to morning pale,
The warriors' yell will sound our wild reveille.

SCENE FOURTH.
TECUMSEH'S CABIN.

Enter IENA.
IENA. Tis night, and Mamatee is absent still!
Why should this sorrow weigh upon my heart,
And other lonely things on earth have rest?
Oh, could I be with them! The lily shone
All day upon the stream, and now it sleeps
Under the wave in peace—in cradle soft
Which sorrow soon may fashion for my grave.
Ye shadows which do creep into my thoughts—
Ye curtains of despair! what is my fault,
That ye should hide the happy earth from me?
Once I had joy of it, when tender Spring,
Mother of beauty, hid me in her leaves;
When Summer led me by the shores of song,
And forests and far-sounding cataracts
Melted my soul with music. I have heard
The rough chill harpings of dismantled woods,
When Fall had stripped them, and have felt a joy

Deeper than ear could lend unto the heart;
And when the Winter from his mountains wild
Looked down on death, and, in the frosty sky,
The very stars seemed hung with icicles,
Then came a sense of beauty calm and cold,
That weaned me from myself, yet knit me still
With kindred bonds to Nature. All is past,
And he—who won from me such love for him,
And he—my valiant uncle and my friend,
Comes not to lift the cloud that drapes my soul,
And shield me from the fiendish Prophet's power.
[Enter MAMATEE.]
Give me his answer in his very words!
MAMATEE. There is a black storm raging in his mind—
His eye darts lightning like the angry cloud
Which hangs in woven darkness o'er the earth.
Brief is his answer—you must go to him.
The Long-Knife's camp fires gleam among the oaks
Which dot yon western hill. A thousand men
Are sleeping there cajoled to fatal dreams
By promises the Prophet breaks to-night. Hark! 'tis the war-song.
IENA. Dares the Prophet now
Betray Tecumseh's trust, and break his faith?
MAMATEE. He dares do anything will feed ambition.
His dancing braves are frenzied by his tongue,
Which prophesies revenge and victory.
Before the break of day he will surprise
The Long-Knife's camp, and hang our people's fate
Upon a single onset.
IENA. Should he fail?
MAMATEE. Then all will fail;—Tecumseh's scheme will fail.
IENA. It shall not! Let us go to him at once!
MAMATEE. And risk your life?
IENA. Risk hovers everywhere
When night and man combine for darksome deeds.
I'll go to him, and argue on my knees—
Yea, yield my hand—would I could give my heart!
To stay his purpose and this act of ruin.
MAMATEE. He is not in the mood for argument
Rash girl! they die who would oppose him now.
IENA. Such death were sweet as life—I go!
But, first—Great Spirit! I commit my soul to Thee.

[Kneels.]

SCENE FIFTH.
AN OPEN SPACE IN THE FOREST NEAR THE PROPHET'S TOWN. A FIRE OF BILLETS BURNING. WAR CRIES ARE HEARD FROM THE TOWN.
Enter the PROPHET.

PROPHET. My spells do work apace! Shout yourselves hoarse,
Ye howling ministers by whom I climb!
For this I've wrought until my weary tongue,
Blistered with incantation, flags in speech,
And half declines its office. Every brave
Inflamed by charms and oracles, is now
A vengeful serpent, who will glide ere morn
To sting the Long-Knife's sleeping camp to death.
Why should I hesitate? My promises!
My duty to Tecumseh! What are these
Compared with duty here? Where I perceive
A near advantage, there my duty lies;
Consideration strong which overweighs
All other reason. Here is Harrison—
Trepanned to dangerous lodgment for the night—
Each deep ravine which grooves the prairie's breast
A channel of approach; each winding creek
A screen for creeping death. Revenge is sick
To think of such advantage flung aside. For what?
To let Tecumseh's greatness grow,
Who gathers his rich harvest of renown
Out of the very fields that I have sown!
By Manitou, I will endure no more!
Nor, in the rising flood of our affairs,
Fish like an osprey for this eagle longer.
But, soft!
It is the midnight hour when comes
Tarhay to claim his bride, (calls) Tarhay!
Tarhay!
[Enter TARHAY with several braves.]
TARHAY. Tarhay is here!
PROPHET. The Long-Knives die to-night.
The spirits which do minister to me
Have breathed this utterance within my ear.

TECUMSEH

You know my sacred office cuts me off
From the immediate leadership in fight.
My nobler work is in the spirit-world,
And thence come promises which make us strong.
Near to the foe I'll keep the Magic Bowl,
Whilst you, Tarhay, shall lead our warriors on.
TARHAY. I'll lead them; they are wild with eagerness.
But fill my cold and empty cabin first
With light and heat! You know I love your niece,
And have the promise of her hand to-night.
PROPHET. She shall be yours!
(To the braves)
Go bring her here at once—But, look! Fulfilment of my promise comes
In her own person.
Enter IENA and MAMATEE.
Welcome, my sweet niece! You have forestalled my message by these braves, And come unbidden to your wedding place.
IENA. Uncle! you know my heart is far away—
PROPHET. But still your hand is here! this little hand! (Pulling her forward)
IENA. Dare you enforce a weak and helpless girl,
Who thought to move you by her misery?
Stand back! I have a message for you too.
What means the war-like song, the dance of braves,
And bustle in our town?
PROPHET. It means that we
Attack the foe to-night.
IENA. And risk our all?
O that Tecumseh knew! his soul would rush
In arms to intercept you. What! break faith,
And on the hazard of a doubtful strife,
Stake his great enterprise and all our lives!
The dying curses of a ruined race
Will wither up your wicked heart for this!
PROPHET. False girl! your heart is with our foes;
Your hand I mean to turn to better use.
IENA. Oh, could it turn you from your mad intent
How freely would I give it! Drop this scheme,
Dismiss your frenzied warriors to their beds;
And, if contented with my hand, Tarhay
Can have it here.
TARHAY. I love you, Iena!

IENA. Then must you love what I do! Love our race!
'Tis this love nerves Tecumseh to unite
Its scattered tribes—his fruit of noble toil,
Which you would snatch unripened from his hand,
And feed to sour ambition. Touch it not—
Oh, touch it not Tarhay! and though my heart
Breaks for it, I am yours.
PROPHET. His anyway,
Or I am not the Prophet!
TARHAY. For my part I have no leaning to this rash attempt,
Since Iena consents to be my wife.
PROPHET. Shall I be thwarted by a yearning fool! (Aside.)
This soft, sleek girl, to outward seeming good,
I know to be a very fiend beneath—
Whose sly affections centre on herself,
And feed the gliding snake within her heart.
TARHAY. I cannot think her so—
MAMATEE. She is not so!
There is the snake that creeps among our race;
Whose venomed fangs would bite into our lives,
And poison all our hopes.
PROPHET. She is the head—
The very neck of danger to me here,
Which I must break at once! (aside)
Tarhay—attend! I can see dreadful visions in the air;
I can dream awful dreams of life and fate;
I can bring darkness on the heavy earth;
I can fetch shadows from our fathers' graves,
And spectres from the sepulchres of hell
Who dares dispute with me, disputes with death! Dost hear, Tarhay?
[TARHAY and braves cower before the PROPHET.]
TARHAY. I hear, and will obey. Spare me! Spare me!
PROPHET. As for this foolish girl,
The hand she offers you on one condition,
I give to you upon a better one;
And, since she has no mind to give her heart
Which, rest assured, is in her body stity
There,—take it at my hands!
Flings IENA violently toward TARHAY, into whose arms she falls fainting, and is then borne away by MAMATEE.

(To TARHAY.) Go bring the braves to view the Mystic Torch
And belt of Sacred Beans grown from my flesh
One touch of it makes them invulnerable
Then creep, like stealthy panthers, on the foe!

SCENE SIXTH.
MORNING. THE FIELD OF TIPPECANOE AFTER THE BATTLE. THE GROUND STREWN WITH DEAD SOLDIERS AND WARRIORS.

Enter HARRISON, officers and soldiers and BARRON.
HARRISON. A costly triumph reckoned by our slain!
Look how some lie still clenched with savages
In all-embracing death, their bloody hands
Glued in each other's hair! Make burial straight
Of all alike in deep and common graves:
Their quarrel now is ended.
1ST OFFICER. I have heard.
The red man fears our steel—'twas not so here;
From the first shots, which drove our pickets in,
Till daylight dawned they rushed upon our lines,
And flung themselves upon our bayonet points
In frenzied recklessness of bravery.
BARRON. They trusted in the Prophet's rites and spells,
Which promised them immunity from death.
All night he sat on yon safe eminence,
Howling his songs of war and mystery,
Then fled, at dawn, in fear of his own braves.
[Enter an AIDE]
HARRISON. What tidings bring you from the Prophet's Town?
AIDE. The wretched women with their children fly
To distant forests for concealment. In
Their village is no living thing save mice
Which scampered as we oped each cabin door.
Their pots still simmered on the vacant hearths,
Standing in dusty silence and desertion.
Naught else we saw, save that their granaries
Were crammed with needful corn.
HARRISON. Go bring it all—
Then burn their village down!
[Exit AIDE.]

2ND OFFICER. This victory
Will shake Tecumseh's project to the base
Were I the Prophet I should drown myself
Rather than meet him.
BARRON. We have news of him—
Our scouts report him near in heavy force.
HARRISON. 'Twill melt or draw across the British line,
And wait for war. But double the night watch,
Lest he should strike, and give an instant care
To all our wounded men: to-morrow's sun
Must light us on our backward march for home
Thence Rumour's tongue will spread so proud a story
New England will grow envious of our glory;
And, greedy for renown so long abhorred,
Will on old England draw the tardy sword!

SCENE SEVENTH.
THE RUINS OF THE PROPHET'S TOWN.

[Enter the PROPHET, who gloomily surveys the place.]
PROPHET. Our people scattered, and our town in ashes!
To think these hands could work such madness here—
This envious head devise this misery!
Tecumseh, had not my ambition drawn
Such sharp and fell destruction on our race
You might have smiled at me! for I have matched
My cunning 'gainst your wisdom, and have dragged
Myself and all into a sea of ruin.
[Enter TECUMSEH.]
TECUMSEH. Devil! I have discovered you at last!
You sum of treacheries, whose wolfish fangs
Have torn our people's flesh—you shall not live!
[The PROPHET retreats facing and followed by TECUMSEH.]
PROPHET. Nay—strike me not! I can explain it all!
It was a woman touched the Magic Bowl,
And broke the brooding spell.
TECUMSEH. Impostor! Slave! Why should I spare you?
[Lifts his hand as if to strike.]
PROPHET. Stay, stay, touch me not!
One mother bore us in the self-same hour.
TECUMSEH. Then good and evil came to light together.
Go to the corn-dance, change your name to villain!
Away! Your presence tempts my soul to mischief.

[Exit the PROPHET hastily.]
Would that I were a woman, and could weep,
And slake hot rage with tears! O spiteful fortune,
To lure me to the limit of my dreams,
Then turn and crowd the ruin of my toil
Into the narrow compass of a night.
My brother's deep disgrace—myself the scorn
Of envious harriers and thieves of fame,
Who fain would rob me of the lawful meed
Of faithful services and duties done—
Oh, I could bear it all! But to behold
Our ruined people hunted to their graves—
To see the Long-Knife triumph in their shame—
This is the burning shaft, the poisoned wound
That rankles in my soul! But, why despair?
All is not lost—the English are our friends.
My spirit rises—manhood bear me up!
I'll haste to Malden, join my force to theirs,
And fall with double fury on our foes.
Farewell ye plains and forests, but rejoice!
Ye yet shall echo to Tecumseh's voice.
[Enter LEFROY.]
LEFROY. What tidings have you gleaned of Iena?
TECUMSEH. My brother meant to wed her to Tarhay—
The chief who led his warriors to ruin;
But, in the gloom and tumult of the night,
She fled into the forest all alone.
LEFROY. Alone! In the wide forest all alone!
Angels are with her now, for she is dead.
TECUMSEH. You know her to be skilful with the bow.
'Tis certain she would strike for some great Lake—
Erie or Michigan. At the Detroit
Are people of our nation, and perchance
She fled for shelter there. I go at once
To join the British force.
[Exit TECUMSEH.]
LEFROY. But yesterday I climbed to Heaven upon the shining stairs
Of love and hope, and here am quite cast down.
My little flower amidst a weedy world,
Where art thou now? In deepest forest shade?
Or onward, where the sumach stands arrayed
In Autumn splendour, its alluring form

Fruited, yet odious with the hidden worm?
Or, farther, by some still sequestered lake,
Loon-haunted, where the sinewy panthers slake
Their noon-day thirst, and never voice is heard
Joyous of singing waters, breeze or bird,
Save their wild waitings.—(A halloo without)
'Tis Tecumseh calls! Oh Iena! If dead, where'er thou art—
Thy saddest grave will be this ruined heart!
[Exit.]

END OF THIRD ACT

ACT IV. TECUMSEH

Enter CHORUS.
War is declared, unnatural and wild,
By Revolution's calculating sons!
So leave the home of mercenary minds,
And wing with me, in your uplifted thoughts,
Away to our unyielding Canada!
There to behold the Genius of the Land,
Beneath her singing pine and sugared tree,
Companioned with the lion, Loyalty.

SCENE FIRST.
A ROOM IN FORT GEORGE.

[Enter GENERAL BROCK reading a despatch from Montreal.]
BROCK. Prudent and politic Sir George Prevost!
Hull's threatened ravage of our western coast,
Hath more breviloquence than your despatch.
Storms are not stilled by reasoning with air,
Nor fires quenched by a syrup of sweet words.
So to the wars, Diplomacy, for now
Our trust is in our arms and arguments
Delivered only from the cannon's mouth!
[Rings.]
[Enter an ORDERLY.]
ORDERLY. Your Exc'llency?
BROCK. Bid Colonel Proctor come!
[Exit Orderly.]

Now might the head of gray Experience
Shake o'er the problems that surround us here.
I am no stranger to the brunt of war,
But all the odds so lean against our side
That valour's self might tremble for the issue,
Could England stretch its full, assisting hand
Then might I smile though velvet-footed time
Struck all his claws at once into our flesh;
But England, noble England, fights for life,
Couching the knightly lance for liberty
'Gainst a new dragon that affrights the world.
And, now, how many noisome elements
Would plant their greed athwart this country's good!
How many demagogues bewray its cause!
How many aliens urge it to surrender!
Our present good must match their present ill,
And, on our frontiers, boldest deeds in war,
Dismay the foe, and strip the loins of faction.
[Enter COLONEL PROCTOR.]
Time waits not our conveniency; I trust
Your preparations have no further needs.
PROCTOR. All is in readiness, and I can leave
For Amherstburg at once.
BROCK. Then tarry not,
For time is precious to us now as powder.
You understand my wishes and commands?
PROCTOR. I know them and shall match them with obedience.
BROCK. Rest not within the limit of instructions
If you can better them, for they should bind
The feeble only; able men enlarge
And shape them to their needs. Much must be done
That lies in your discretion. At Detroit
Hull vaunts his strength, and meditates invasion,
And loyalty, unarmed, defenceless, bare,
May let this boaster light upon our shores
Without one manly motion of resistance.
So whilst I open Parliament at York,
Close it again, and knit our volunteers,
Be yours the task to head invasion off.
Act boldly, but discreetly, and so draw
Our interest to the balance, that affairs
May hang in something like an even scale,
Till I can join you with a fitting force,

And batter this old Hull until he sinks.
So fare-you-well—success attend your mission!
PROCTOR. Farewell, sir! I shall do my best in this,
And put my judgment to a prudent use
In furtherance of all.
[Exit PROCTOR.]
BROCK. Prudent he will be—'tis a vice in him.
For in the qualities of every mind
There's one o'ergrows, and prudence in this man
Tops all the rest. 'Twill suit our present needs.
But, boldness, go with me! for, if I know
My nature well, I shall do something soon
Whose consequence will make the nation cheer,
Or hiss me to my grave.
[Re-enter ORDERLY.]
ORDERLY. Your Exc'llency,
Some settlers wait without.
BROCK. Whence do they come?
[Enter COLONEL MACDONELL.]
ORDERLY. From the raw clearings up Lake Erie, Sir.
BROCK. Go bring them here at once. [Exit
ORDERLY.] The very men Who meanly shirk their service to the crown!
A breach of duty to be remedied,
For disaffection like an ulcer spreads
Until the caustic ointment of the law,
Sternly applied, eats up and stays corruption.
[(Enter DEPUTATION OF YANKEE SETTLERS).]
Good morrow, worthy friends; I trust you bear
Good hopes in loyal hearts for Canada.
1ST SETTLER. That kind o' crop's a failure in our county.
Gen'ral, we came to talk about this war
With the United States. It ain't quite fair
To call out settlers from the other side.
BROCK. From it yet on it too! Why came you thence?
Is land so scarce in the United States?
Are there no empty townships, wilds or wastes
In all their borders but you must encroach
On ours? And, being here, how dare you make
Your dwelling-places harbours of sedition
And furrow British soil with alien ploughs
To feed our enemies? There is not scope,

Not room enough in all this wilderness
For men so base.
2ND SETTLER. Why, General, we thought You wanted settlers here.
BROCK. Settlers indeed
But with the soldier's courage to defend
The land of their adoption. This attack
On Canada is foul and unprovoked;
The hearts are vile, the hands are traitorous
That will not help to hurl invasion back.
Beware the lariat of the law! 'Tis thrown
With aim so true in Canada it brings
Sedition to the ground at every cast.
1ST SETTLER. Well, General, we're not your British
sort,
But if we were we know that Canada
Is naught compared with the United States.
We have no faith in her, but much in them.
BROCK. You have no faith! Then take a creed from me!
For I believe in Britain's Empire, and
In Canada, its true and loyal son,
Who yet shall rise to greatness, and shall stand
At England's shoulder helping her to guard
True liberty throughout a faithless world.
Here is a creed for arsenals and camps,
For hearts and heads that seek their country's good;
So, go at once, and meditate on it!
I have no time to parley with you now—
But think on this as well! that traitors, spies,
And aliens who refuse to take up arms,
Forfeit their holdings, and must leave this land,
Or dangle nearer Heaven than they wish.
So to your homes, and ponder your condition.
[Exeunt Settlers ruefully.]
This foreign element will hamper us.
Its alien spirit ever longs for change,
And union with the States.
MACDONELL. O fear it not,
Nor magnify the girth of noisy men!
Their name is faction, and their numbers few.
While everywhere encompassing them stands
The silent element that doth not change;
That points with steady finger to the Crown—
True as the needle to the viewless pole,

And stable as its star!
BROCK. I know it well,
And trust to it alone for earnestness,
Accordant counsels, loyalty and faith.
But give me these—and let the Yankees come!
With our poor handful of inhabitants,
We can defend our forest wilderness,
And spurn the bold invader from our shores.
[Re-enter ORDERLY.]
ORDERLY. Your boat is ready, sir!
BROCK. Man it at once—I shall forthwith to York.
[Exeunt.]

SCENE SECOND.
YORK THE CAPITAL OF UPPER CANADA. THE SPACE IN FRONT OF OLD GOVERNMENT HOUSE.

[Enter two U. E. LOYALISTS, separately.]
1ST U.E. LOYALIST. Well met, my friend! A stirrer like myself.
2ND U. E. LOYALIST. Yes, affairs make me so. Such stirring times Since Brock returned and opened Parliament! Read you his speech?
1ST U. E. LOYALIST. That from the Throne?
2ND U.E. LOYALIST. Ay, that!
1ST U.E. LOYALIST. You need not ask, since 'tis on
every tongue,
Unstaled by repetition. I affirm
Words never showered upon more fruitful soil
To nourish valour's growth.
2ND U. E. LOYALIST. That final phrase—
Oh it struck home: a sentence to be framed
And hung in every honourable heart
For daily meditation.
"We are engaged in an awful and eventful contest. By unanimity and dispatch in our councils, and by vigour in our operations, we may teach the enemy this lesson, that a country defended by free men, enthusiastically devoted to the cause of their king and constitution, can never be conquered."
1ST U. E. LOYALIST. That reaches far; a text to fortify
Imperial doctrine and Canadian rights.
Sedition skulks, and feels its blood a-cold,
Since first it fell upon the public ear.
2ND U. E. LOYALIST. There is a magic in this soldier's
tongue.

O language is a common instrument;
But when a master touches it—what sounds!
1ST U. E. LOYALIST. What sounds indeed!
But Brock can use his sword
Still better than his tongue. Our state affairs,
Conned and digested by his eager mind
Draw into form, and even now his voice
Cries, Forward! To the Front!
2ND U. E. LOYALIST. Look—here he comes!
1ST U.E. LOYALIST. There's matter in the wind; let's draw a-near.
[Enter GENERAL BROCK, accompanied by MACDONELL, NICHOL,
ROBINSON and other Canadian Officers and friends conversing.]
BROCK. 'Tis true our Province faces heavy odds:
Of regulars but fifteen hundred men
To guard a frontier of a thousand miles;
Of volunteers what aidance we can draw
From seventy thousand widely scattered souls.
A meagre showing 'gainst the enemy's
If numbers be the test. But odds lie not
In numbers only, but in spirit too—
Witness the might of England's little isle!
And what made England great will keep her so—
The free soul and the valour of her sons;
And what exalts her will sustain you now
If you contain her courage and her faith.
So not the odds so much are to be feared
As private disaffection, treachery—
Those openers of the door to enemies—
And the poor crouching spirit that gives way
Ere it is forced to yield.
ROBINSON. No fear of that!
BROCK. I trust there is not; yet I speak of it
As what is to be feared more than the odds.
For like to forests are communities—
Fair at a distance, entering you find
The rubbish and the underbrush of states,
'Tis ever the mean soul that counts the odds,
And, where you find this spirit, pluck it up—
'Tis full of mischief.
MACDONELL. It is almost dead.
England's vast war, our weakness, and the eagle
Whetting his beak at Sandwich, with one claw
Already in our side, put thought to steep

In cold conjecture for a time, and gave
A text to alien tongues. But, since you came,
Depression turns to smiling, and men see
That dangers well-opposed may be subdued
Which shunned would overwhelm us.
BROCK. Hold to this!
For since the storm has struck us we must face it.
What is our present count of volunteers?
NICHOL. More than you called for have assembled, Sir—
The flower of York and Lincoln.
BROCK. Some will go
To guard our frontier at Niagara.
Which must be strengthened even at the cost
Of York itself. The rest to the Detroit,
Where, with Tecumseh's force, our regulars,
And Kent and Essex loyal volunteers,
We'll give this Hull a taste of steel so cold
His teeth will chatter at it, and his scheme
Of easy conquest vanish into air.
[Enter a COMPANY of MILITIA with their OFFICERS, unarmed. They salute, march across the stage, and make their exit.]
What men are those? Their faces are familiar.
ROBINSON. Some farmers whom you furloughed at Fort George,
To tend their fields, which still they leave half-reaped
To meet invasion.
BROCK. I remember it!
The jarring needs of harvest-time and war,
Twixt whose necessities grave hazards lay.
ROBINSON. They only thought to save their children's bread,
And then return to battle with light hearts.
For, though their hard necessities o'erpoised
Their duty for the moment, these are men.
Who draw their pith from loyal roots, their sires,
Dug up by revolution, and cast out
To hovel in the bitter wilderness,
And wring, with many a tussle, from the wolf
Those very fields which cry for harvesters.
BROCK. O I observed them closely at Fort George—
Red-hot for action in their summer-sleeves,
And others drilling in their naked feet—

Our poor equipment (which disgraced us there)
Too scanty to go round. See they get arms,
An ample outfit and good quarters too.
NICHOL. They shall be well provided for in all.
[Enter COLONELS BABY [Footnote: Pronounced Baw- bee.] and ELLIOTT.]
BROCK. Good morning both; what news from home, Baby?
BABY. None, none your Excellency—whereat we fear
This Hull is in our rear at Amherstburg.
BROCK. Not yet; what I unsealed last night reports
Tecumseh to have foiled the enemy
In two encounters at the Canard bridge.
A noble fellow; as I hear, humane,
Lofty and bold and rooted in our cause.
BABY. I know him well; a chief of matchless force.
If Mackinaw should fall—that triple key
To inland seas and teeming wilderness—
The bravest in the west will flock to him.
BROCK. 'Twere well he had an inkling of affairs.
My letters say he chafes at my delay,
Not mine, but thine, thou dull and fatuous House—
Which, in a period that whips delay,
When men should spur themselves and flash in action,
Let'st idly leak the unpurchasable hours
From our scant measure of most precious time!
BABY. 'Tis true, Your Exc'llency, some cankered minds
Have been a daily hind'rance in our House.
No measure so essential, bill so fair,
But they would foul it by some cunning clause,
Wrenching the needed statute from its aim
By sly injection of their false opinion.
But this you cannot charge to us whose hearts
Are faithful to our trust; nor yet delay;
For, Exc'llency, you hurry on so fast
That other men wheeze after, out of breath,
And haste itself, disparaged, lags behind.
BROCK. Friends, pardon me, you stand not in reproof.
But haste, the evil of the age in peace,
Is war's auxiliary, confederate
With time himself in urgent great affairs.
So must we match it with the flying hours!
I shall prorogue this tardy Parliament,
And promptly head our forces for Detroit

Meanwhile, I wish you, in advance of us,
To speed unto your homes. Spread everywhere
Throughout the West, broad tidings of our coming,
Which, by the counter currents of reaction,
Will tell against our foes and for our friends.
As for the rest, such loyal men as you
Need not our counsel; so, good journey both!
BABY. We shall not spare our transport or ourselves.
[Enter a travel-stained MESSENGER.]
ELLIOTT. Good-bye.
BABY. Tarry a moment, Elliott! Here comes a messenger— let's have his news.
MESSENGER. It is his Excellency whom I seek. I come, sir, with despatches from the west.
BROCK. Tidings I trust to strengthen all our hopes.
MESSENGER. News of grave interest, this not the worst.
[Handing a letter to GENERAL BROCK.]
BROCK. No, by my soul, for Mackinaw is ours!
That vaunted fort, whose gallant capture frees
Our red allies. This is important news! What of
Detroit!
MESSENGER. Things vary little there.
Hull's soldiers scour our helpless settlements,
Our aliens join them, but the loyal mass—
Sullen, yet overawed, longs for relief.
BROCK. I hope to better this anon. You, sirs,
[To his aides.]
Come with me; here is matter to despatch
At once to Montreal. Farewell, my friends.
[To Baby and Elliott.]
BABY. We feel now what will follow this, farewell!
[Exeunt BABY, ELLIOTT and MESSENGER.]
BROCK. Now, gentlemen, prepare against our needs,
That no neglect may check us at the start,
Or mar our swift advance. And, for our cause,
As we believe it just in sight of God,
So should it triumph in the sight of man,
Whose generous temper, at the first, assigns
Right to the weaker side, yet coldly draws
Damning conclusions from its failure. Now
Betake you to your tasks with double zeal;
And, meanwhile, let our joyful tidings spread!
[Exeunt.]

SCENE THIRD.
THE SAME.

Enter two OLD MEN of York, severally.
1ST OLD MAN. Good morrow, friend! a fair and fitting time
To take our airing, and to say farewell.
'Tis here, I think, we bid our friends God-speed,
A waftage, peraventure, to their graves.
2ND OLD MAN. 'Tis a good cause they die for, if they fall
By this grey pate, if I were young again,
I would no better journey. Young again!
This hubbub sets old pulses on the bound
As I were in my teens.
Enter a CITIZEN.
What news afoot?
CITIZEN. Why everyone's afoot and coming here.
York's citizens are turned to warriors;
The learned professions go a-soldiering,
And gentle hearts beat high for Canada!
For, as you pass, on every hand you see,
Through the neglected openings of each house—
Through doorways, windows—our Canadian maids
Strained by their parting lovers to their breasts;
And loyal matrons busy round their lords,
Buckling their arms on, or, with tearful eyes,
Kissing them to the war!
1ST OLD MAN. The volunteers Will pass this way?
CITIZEN. Yes, to the beach, and there
Embark for Burlington, whence they will march
To Long Point, taking open boats again,
To plough the shallow Erie's treacherous flood.
Such leaky craft as farmers market with:
Rare bottoms, one sou-wester-driven wave
Would heave against Lake Erie's wall of shore,
And dash to fragments. 'Tis an awful hazard—
A danger which in apprehension lies,
Yet palpable unto the spirit's touch,
As earth to finger.
1ST OLD MAN. Let us hope a calm May lull this fretful and ill-tempered lake Whilst they ascend.

[Military music is heard.]
CITIZEN. Hark! here our soldiers come.
Enter GENERAL BROCK, with his aides, MACDONELL and GLEGG, NICHOL, and other Officers, followed by the Volunteers in companies. A concourse of citizens.
MACDONELL. Our fellows show the mark of training, sir,
And many, well in hand, yet full of fire,
Are burning for distinction.
BROCK. This is good: Love of distinction is the fruitful soil
From which brave actions spring; and, superposed
On love of country, these strike deeper root,
And grow to greater greatness. Cry a halt—
A word here—then away!
[Flourish. The volunteers halt, form line, and order arms.]
Ye men of Canada! Subjects with me of that Imperial Power
Whose liberties are marching round the earth:
I need not urge you now to follow me,
Though what befalls will try your stubborn faith
In the fierce fire and crucible of war.
I need not urge you, who have heard the voice
Of loyalty, and answered to its call.
Who has not read the insults of the foe—
The manifesto of his purposed crimes?
That foe, whose poison-plant, false-liberty,
Runs o'er his body politic and kills
Whilst seeming to adorn it, fronts us now!
Threats our poor Province to annihilate,
And should he find the red men by our side—
Poor injured souls, who but defend their own—
Calls black Extermination from its hell,
To stalk abroad, and stench your land with slaughter.
These are our weighty arguments for war,
Wherein armed justice will enclasp its sword,
And sheath it in its bitter adversary;
Wherein we'll turn our bayonet-points to pens,
And write in blood:—Here lies the poor invader;
Or be ourselves struck down by hailing death;
Made stepping-stones for foes to walk upon—
The lifeless gangways to our country's ruin.
For now we look not with the eye of fear;
We reck not if this strange mechanic frame—

Stop in an instant in the shock of war.
Our death may build into our country's life,
And failing this, 'twere better still to die
Than live the breathing spoils of infamy.
Then forward for our cause and Canada!
Forward for Britain's Empire—peerless arch
Of Freedom's raising, whose majestic span
Is axis to the world! On, on, my friends!
The task our country sets must we perform—
Wring peace from war, or perish in its storm!
[Excitement and leave-taking. The volunteers break into column and sing:]
O hark to the voice from the lips of the free!
O hark to the cry from the lakes to the sea!
Arm! arm! the invader is wasting our coasts,
And tainting the air of our land with his hosts.
Arise! then, arise! let us rally and form,
And rush like the torrent, and sweep like the storm,
On the foes of our King,—of our country adored,
Of the flag that was lost, but in exile restored!
And whose was the flag? and whose was the soil?
And whose was the exile, the suffering, the toil?
Our Fathers'! who carved in the forest a name,
And left us rich heirs of their freedom and fame.
Oh, dear to our hearts is that flag, and the land
Our Fathers bequeathed—'tis the work of their hand!
And the soil they redeemed from the woods with renown
The might of their sons will defend for the Crown!
Our hearts they are one, and our hands they are free,
From clime unto clime, and from sea unto sea!
And chaos will come to the States that annoy,
But our Empire united what foe can destroy?
Then away! to the front! march! comrades away!
In the lists of each hour crowd the work of a day!
We will follow our leader to fields far and nigh,
And for Canada fight, and for Canada die!
[Exeunt with military music.]

SCENE FOURTH.
FORT DETROIT.—THE AMERICAN CAMP.

Enter GENERAL HULL, COLONEL CASS and other Officers.
CASS. Come, General, we must insist on reasons!
Your order to withdraw from Canada

Will blow to mutiny, and put to shame
That proclamation which I wrote for you,
Wherein 'tis proudly said, "We are prepared
To look down opposition, our strong force
But vanguard of a mightier still to come!"
And men have been attracted to our cause
Who now will curse us for this breach of faith.
Consider, sir, again!
HULL. I am not bound
To tack my reasons to my orders; this
Is my full warrant and authority—
[Pointing to his Instructions.]
Yet, I have ample grounds for what I do.
CASS. What are they, then?
HULL. First, that this proclamation
Meets not with due response, wins to our side
The thief and refugee, not honest men.
These plainly rally round their government.
1ST OFFICER. Why, yes; there's something lacking in this people, If we must conquer them to set them free.
HULL. Ay, and our huge force must be larger still,
If we would change these Provinces to States.
Then, Colonel Proctor's intercepted letter—
Bidding the captor of Fort Mackinaw
Send but five thousand warriors from the West,
Which, be it artifice or not, yet points
To great and serious danger.
Add to this Brock's rumoured coming with his
Volunteers, All burning to avenge their fathers' wrongs,
And our great foe, Tecumseh, fired o'er his;
These are the reasons; grave enough, I think,
Which urge me to withdraw from Canada,
And wait for further force; so, go at once,
And help our soldiers to recross the river.
CASS. But I see——
HULL. No "buts"! You have my orders.
CASS. No solid reason here, naught but a group
Of flimsy apprehensions——
HULL. Go at once!
Who kicks at judgment, lacks it.
CASS. I——
HULL. No more! I want not wrangling but obedience here.

[Exeunt CASS and other officers incensed.]
Would I had ne'er accepted this command!
Old men are out of favour with the time,
And youthful folly scoffs at hoary age.
There's not a man who executes my orders
With a becoming grace; not one but sulks,
And puffs his disapproval with a frown.
And what am I? A man whom Washington
Nodded approval of, and wrote it too!
Yet here, in judgment and discretion both,
Ripe to the dropping, scorned and ridiculed.
Oh, Jefferson, what mischief have you wrought—
Confounding Nature's order, setting fools
To prank themselves, and sit in wisdom's seat
By right divine, out Heroding a King's!
But I shall keep straight on—pursue my course,
Responsible and with authority,
Though boasters gird at me, and braggarts frown.
[Exit.]

SCENE FIFTH.
SANDWICH, ON THE DETROIT.—A ROOM IN THE BABY MANSION.

Enter GENERAL BROCK, COLONELS PROCTOR, GLEGG, BABY, MACDONELL, NICHOL, ELLIOTT and other Officers.
BABY. Welcome! thrice welcome!
Brave Brock, to Sandwich and this loyal roof!
Thank God, your oars, those weary levers bent
In many a wave, have been unshipped at last;
And, now methinks those lads who stemmed the flood
Would boldly face the fire.
BROCK. I never led
Men of more cheerful and courageous heart,
But for whose pluck, foul weather and short seas,
'Twere truth to say, had made an end of us.
Another trial will, I think, approve
The manly strain this Canada hath bred.
PROCTOR. 'Tis pity that must be denied them now,
Since all our enemies have left our shores.
BROCK. No, by my soul, it shall not be denied!
Our foe's withdrawal hath a magnet's power
And pulls my spirit clean into his fort.

But I have asked you to confer on this.
What keeps Tecumseh?
ELLIOTT. 'Tis his friend, Lefroy,
Who now rejoins him, after bootless quest
Of Iena, Tecumseh's niece.
BROCK. Lefroy! I had a gentle playmate of that name
In Guernsey, long ago.
BABY. It may be he.
I know him, and, discoursing our affairs,
Have heard him speak of you, but in a strain
Peculiar to the past.
BROCK. He had in youth.
All goods belonging to the human heart,
But fell away to Revolution's side—
Impulsive ever, and o'er prompt to see
In kings but tyrants, and in laws but chains.
I have not seen or heard of him for years.
BABY. The very man!
BROCK. 'Tis strange to find him here!
ELLIOTT. He calls the red men freedom's last survival;
Says truth is only found in Nature's growth—
Her first intention, ere false knowledge rose
To frame distinctions, and exhaust the world.
BROCK. Few find like him the substance of their dreams. But, Elliott, let us seek Tecumseh now. Stay, friends, till we return.
[Exeunt BROCK and ELLIOTT.]
GLEGG. How odd to find
An old friend in this fashion!
PROCTOR. Humph! a fool
Who dotes on forest tramps and savages.
Why, at the best, they are the worst of men;
And this Tecumseh has so strained my temper,
So over-stept my wishes, thrid my orders,
That I would sooner ask the devil's aid
Than such as his.
NICHOL. Why, Brock is charmed with him!
And, as you saw, at Amherstburg he put
Most stress upon opinion when he spoke.
MACDONELL. Already they've determined on assault.
PROCTOR. Then most unwisely so! There are no bounds
To this chief's rashness, and our General seem
Swayed by it too, or rashness hath a twin.
NICHOL. Well, rashness is the wind of enterprise,

And blows its banners out. But here they come
Who dig beneath their rashness for their reasons.
Re-enter GENERAL BROCK and COLONEL ELLIOTT, accompanied by TECUMSEH, conversing.
TECUMSEH. We have been much abused! and have abused
Our fell destroyers too—making our wrongs
The gauge of our revenge. And, still forced back
From the first justice and the native right,
Ever revenge hath sway. This we would void,
And, by a common boundary, prevent.
So, granting that a portion of our own
Is still our own, then let that portion be
Confirmed by sacred treaty to our tribes.
This is my sum of asking—you have ears!
BROCK. Nay, then, Tecumseh, speak of it no more!
My promise is a pledge, and from a man
Who never turned his back on friend or foe.
The timely service you have done our cause,
Rating not what's to come, would warrant it.
So, if I live, possess your soul of this—
No treaty for a peace, if we prevail,
Will bear a seal that doth not guard your rights.
Here, take my sash, and wear it for my sake—
Tecumseh can esteem a soldier's gift.
TECUMSEH. Thanks, thanks, my brother,
I have faith in you;
My life is at your service!
BROCK. Gentlemen, Have you considered my proposal well
Touching the capture of Detroit by storm? What say you
Colonel Proctor?
PROCTOR. I object! 'Tis true, the enemy has left our shores,
But what a sorry argument is this!
For his withdrawal, which some sanguine men,
Jumping all other motives, charge to fear,
Prudence, more deeply searching, lays to craft.
Why should a foe, who far outnumbers us,
Retreat o'er this great river, save to lure
Our poor force after him? And, having crossed—
Our weakness seen, and all retreat cut off—
What would ensue but absolute surrender,
Or sheer destruction? 'Tis too hazardous!
Discretion balks at such a mad design.

BROCK. What say the rest?
1ST OFFICER. I fear 'tis indiscreet.
2ND OFFICER. 'Twould be imprudent with our scanty force.
BROCK. What say you, Nichol, to my foolish scheme?
NICHOL. I think it feasible and prudent too.
Hull's letters, captured by Tecumseh, prove
His soldiers mutinous, himself despondent.
And dearly Rumor loves the wilderness,
Which gives a thousand echoes to a tongue
That ever swells and magnifies our strength.
And in this flux we take him, on the hinge
Of two uncertainties—his force and ours.
So, weighed, objections fall; and our attempt,
Losing its grain of rashness, takes its rise
In clearest judgment, whose effect will nerve
All Canada to perish, ere she yield.
BROCK. My very thoughts! What says Tecumseh now?
TECUMSEH. I say attack the fort! This very night I'll cross my braves, if you decide on this.
BROCK. Then say no more! Glegg, take a flag of truce,
And bear to Hull this summons to surrender.
Tell him Tecumseh and his force are here—
A host of warriors brooding on their wrongs,
Who, should resistance flush them to revenge,
Would burst from my control like wind-borne fire,
And match on earth the miseries of hell.
But, should he yield, his safety is assured.
Tell him Tecumseh's word is pledged to this,
Who, though his temperate will in peace is law
Yet casts a loose rein to enforced rage.
Add what your fancy dictates; but the stress
Place most on what I speak of—this he fears,
And these same fears, well wrought upon by you,
May prove good workers for us yet.
GLEGG. I go, And shall acquit myself as best I can.
[Exit GLEGG.]
BROCK. Tecumseh, wonder not at such a message!
The guilty conscience of your foes is judge
Of their deserts, and hence 'twill be believed.
The answer may be 'nay,' so to our work—
Which perfected, we shall confer again,
Then cross at break of morn.
[Exeunt all but TECUMSEH.]

TECUMSEH. This is a man!
And our great father, waking from his sleep,
Has sent him to oar aid. Master of Life,
Endue my warriors with double strength!
May the wedged helve be faithful to the axe,
The arrow fail not, and the flint be firm!
That our great vengeance, like the whirlwind fell,
May cleave through thickets of our enemies
A broad path to our ravaged lands again.
[Exit.]

SCENE SIXTH.
MOONLIGHT. THE BANK OF THE DETROIT RIVER, NEAR THE BABY MANSION.

Enter CAPTAIN ROBINSON.
ROBINSON. I thought to find my brother here—poor boy,
The day's hard labor woos him to his rest.
How sweet the night! how beautiful the place!
Who would not love thee, good old Sandwich town!
Abode of silence and sweet summer dreams—
Let speculation pass, nor progress touch
Thy silvan homes with hard, unhallowed hand!
The light wind whispers, and the air is rich
With vapours which exhale into the night;
And, round me here, this village in the leaves
Darkling doth slumber. How those giant pears
Loom with uplifted and high-ancient heads,
Like forest trees! A hundred years ago
They, like their owner, had their roots in France—
In fruitful Normandy—but here refuse
Unlike, to multiply, as if their spirits
Grieved in their alien home. The village sleeps,
So should I seek that hospitable roof
Of thine, thou good old loyalist, Baby!
Thy mansion is a shrine, whereto shall come
On pilgrimages, in the distant days,
The strong and generous youths of Canada,
And, musing there in rich imaginings,
Restore the balance and the beaver-pack
To the wide hall; see forms of savagery,
Vanished for ages, and the stately shades
Of great Tecumseh and high-hearted Brock.

So shall they profit, drinking of the past,
And, drinking loyally, enlarge the faith
Which love of country breeds in noble minds.
But now to sleep—good night unto the world!
[Exit.]

SCENE SEVENTH.
THE SAME.

Enter IENA, in distress.
IENA. Oh, have I eaten of the spirit-plant!
My head swims, and my senses are confused,
And all grows dark around me. Where am I?
Alas! I know naught save of wanderings,
And this poor bosom's weight. What pang is here,
Which all my pressing cannot ease away?
Poor heart! poor heart! Oh, I have travelled far,
And in the forest's brooding place, or where
Night-shrouded surges beat on lonely shores,
Have sickened with my deep, dread, formless fears;
But, never have I felt what now I feel!
Great Spirit, hear me! help me!—this is death!
[_Staggers and swoons behind some shrubbery._]
Enter_ GENERAL BROCK and LEFROY.
BROCK. You may be right, Lefroy! but, for my part,
I stand by old tradition and the past.
My father's God is wise enough for me,
And wise enough this grey world's wisest men.
LEFROY. I tell you, Brock,
The world is wiser than its wisest men,
And shall outlive the wisdom of its gods
Made after man's own liking. The crippled throne
No longer shelters the uneasy king,
And outworn sceptres and imperial crowns
Now grow fantastic as an idiot's dream.
These perish with the kingly pastime, war,
And war's blind tool, the monster, Ignorance!
Both hateful in themselves, but this the worst.
One tyrant will remain—one impious fiend.
Whose name is Gold—our earliest, latest foe!
Him must the earth destroy, ere man can rise,
Rightly self made, to his high destiny,
Purged of his grossest faults; humane and kind;

Co-equal with his fellows, and as free.
BROCK. Lefroy, such thoughts, let loose, would wreck the world.
The kingly function is the soul of state,
The crown the emblem of authority,
And loyalty the symbol of all faith.
Omitting these, man's government decays—
His family falls into revolt and ruin.
But let us drop this bootless argument,
And tell me more of those unrivalled wastes
You and Tecumseh visited.
LEFROY. We left
The silent forest, and, day after day,
Great prairies swept beyond our aching sight
Into the measureless West; uncharted realms,
Voiceless and calm, save when tempestuous wind
Rolled the rank herbage into billows vast,
And rushing tides, which never found a shore.
And tender clouds, and veils of morning mist
Cast flying shadows, chased by flying light,
Into interminable wildernesses,
Flushed with fresh blooms, deep perfumed by the rose,
And murmurous with flower-fed bird and bee.
The deep-grooved bison-paths like furrows lay,
Turned by the cloven hoofs of thundering herds
Primeval, and still travelled as of yore.
And gloomy valleys opened at our feet—
Shagged with dusk cypresses and hoary pine;
And sunless gorges, rummaged by the wolf,
Which through long reaches of the prairie wound,
Then melted slowly into upland vales,
Lingering, far-stretched amongst the spreading hills.
BROCK. What charming solitudes! And life was there!
LEFROY. Yes, life was there! inexplicable life,
Still wasted by inexorable death.
There had the stately stag his battle-field—
Dying for mastery among his hinds.
There vainly sprung the affrighted antelope,
Beset by glittering eyes and hurrying feet.
The dancing grouse at their insensate sport,
Heard not the stealthy footstep of the fox;
The gopher on his little earthwork stood,
With folded arms, unconscious of the fate

That wheeled in narrowing circles overhead,
And the poor mouse, on heedless nibbling bent,
Marked not the silent coiling of the snake.
At length we heard a deep and solemn sound—
Erupted moanings of the troubled earth
Trembling beneath innumerable feet.
A growing uproar blending in our ears,
With noise tumultuous as ocean's surge,
Of bellowings, fierce breath and battle shock,
And ardor of unconquerable herds.
A multitude whose trampling shook the plains,
With discord of harsh sound and rumblings deep,
As if the swift revolving earth had struck,
And from some adamantine peak recoiled—
Jarring. At length we topped a high-browed hill—
The last and loftiest of a file of such—
And, lo! before us lay the tameless stock,
Slow-wending to the northward like a cloud!
A multitude in motion, dark and dense—
Far as the eye could reach, and farther still,
In countless myriads stretched for many a league.
BROCK. You fire me with the picture! What a scene!
LEFROY. Nation on nation was invillaged there,
Skirting the flanks of that imbanded host;
With chieftains of strange speech and port of war,
Who, battle-armed, in weather-brawny bulk,
Roamed fierce and free in huge and wild content.
These gave Tecumseh greetings fair and kind,
Knowing the purpose havened in his soul.
And he, too, joined the chase as few men dare;
For I have seen him, leaping from his horse,
Mount a careering bull in foaming flight,
Urge it to fury o'er its burden strange,
Yet cling tenacious, with a grip of steel,
Then, by a knife-plunge, fetch it to its knees
In mid-career, and pangs of speedy death.
BROCK. You rave, Lefroy! or saw this in a dream.
LEFROY. No, no; 'tis true—I saw him do it, Brock!
Then would he seek the old, and with his spoils
Restore them to the bounty of their youth,
Cheering the crippled lodge with plenteous feasts,
And warmth of glossy robes, as soft as down,
'Till withered cheeks ran o'er with feeble smiles,

And tongues, long silent, babbled of their prime.
BROCK. This warrior's fabric is of perfect parts!
A worthy champion of his race—he heaps
Such giant obligations on our heads
As will outweigh repayment. It is late,
And rest must preface war's hot work to-morrow,
Else would I talk till morn. How still the night!
Here Peace has let her silvery tresses down,
And falls asleep beside the lapping wave. Wilt go with me?
LEFROY. Nay, I shall stay awhile.
BROCK. You know my quarters and the countersign—
Good-night, Lefroy!
LEFROY. Good-night, good-night, good friend!
[Exit BROCK.]
Give me the open sleep, whose bed is earth,
With airy ceiling pinned by golden stars,
Or vaultage more confined, plastered with clouds!
Your log-roofed barrack-sleep, 'twixt drum and drum,
Suits men who dream of death, and not of love.
Love cannot die, nor its exhausted life,
Exhaling like a breath into the air,
Blend with the universe again. It lives,
Knit to its soul forever. Iena!
Dead in the forest wild—earth cannot claim
Aught but her own from thee. Sleep on! sleep on!
IENA. (Reviving) What place is this?
LEFROY. Who's there? What voice is that!
IENA. Where am I now?
LEFROY. I'll follow up that sound!
A desperate hope now ventures in my heart!
IENA. Help me, kind Spirit!
LEFROY. I could pick that voice
From out a choir of angels! Iena!
[Finds her behind the shrubbery.]
'Tis she! 'tis she! Speak to me, Iena—
No earthly power can mar your life again,
For I am here to shield it with my own.
IENA. Lefroy!
LEFROY. Yes, he!
IENA. My friends! found, found at last!
LEFROY. Found, found my love! I swear it on your lips,
And seal love's contract there! Again—again—

Ah me! all earthly pleasure is a toil
Compared with one long look upon your face.
IENA. O, take me to my friends! A faintness came
Upon me, and no farther could I go.
LEFROY. What spirit led you here?
IENA. My little bark
Is yonder by the shore—but take me hence!
For I am worn and weak with wandering.
LEFROY. Come with me then.
Enter the PROPHET, who stalks gloomily across the stage—scowling at IENA and LEFROY as he passes out.
IENA. The Prophet! I am lost!
LEFROY. This monster here! But he is powerless now.
Fear him not, Iena! Tecumseh's wrath
Burns 'gainst him still—he dare not do thee hurt.
IENA. Must I endure for ever this fiend's hate?
He stabbed me with his eye—
[Swoons away.]
LEFROY. O, horrible! Let us but meet again, and I shall send
His curst soul out of this accursed world!
[Exit LEFROY, carrying IENA.]

SCENE EIGHTH.
THE HIGHWAY THROUGH THE FOREST LEADING TO FORT DETROIT—THE FORT IN THE DISTANCE; CANNON AND GUNNERS AT THE GATE.

Enter TECUMSEH, STAYETA, and other Chiefs and Warriors.
TECUMSEH. There is the Long-Knive's fort, within whose walls
We lose our lives, or find our lands to-day.
Fight for that little space—'tis wide domain!
That small enclosure shuts us from our homes.
There are the victors in the Prophet's strife—
Within that fort they lie—those bloody men
Who burnt your town, to light their triumph up,
And drove your women to the withered woods
To shudder through the cold slow-creeping night,
And help their infants to out-howl the wolf.
Oh, the base Long-Knife grows to head, not heart—
A pitiless and murdering minister
To his desires! But let us now be strong,

And, if we conquer, merciful as strong!
Swoop like the eagles on their prey, but turn
In victory your taste to that of doves;
For ever it has been reproach to us
That we have stained our deeds with cruelty,
And dyed our axes in our captives' blood.
So, here, retort not on a vanquished foe,
But teach him lessons in humanity.
Now let the big heart, swelling in each breast,
Strain every rib for lodgment! Warriors!
Bend to your sacred task, and follow me.
STAYETA. Lead on! We follow you!
KICKAPOO CHIEF. Advance ye braves!
TECUMSEH. Stay! make a circuit in the open woods—
Cross, and recross, and double on the path—
So shall the Long-Knives overcount our strength.
Do this, Stayeta, whilst I meet my friend—
My brave white brother, and confer with him.
Enter GENERAL BROCK, PROCTOR, NICHOL, MACDONELL and other Officers and Forces, on the highway. TECUMSEH goes down to meet them.
BROCK. Now by God's providence we face Detroit,
Either to sleep within its walls to-night,
Or in deep beds dug by exulting foes.
Go, Nichol, make a swift reconnaissance—
We'll follow on.
NICHOL. I shall, but, ere I go I do entreat you,
General, take the rear;
Those guns are shrewdly placed without the gate—
One raking fire might rob us of your life,
And, this lost, all is lost.
BROCK. Well meant, my friend!
But I am here to lead, not follow, men
Whose confidence has come with me thus far!
Go, Nichol, to your task!
[Exit NICHOL. TECUMSEH advances.]
Tecumseh, hail! Brave chieftain, you have made your promise good.
TECUMSEH. My brother stands to his! and I but wait
His orders to advance—my warriors
Are ripe for the assault.
BROCK. Deploy them, then,
Upon our landward flank, and skirt the woods,
Whilst we advance in column to attack.

[TECUMSEH rejoins his warriors.]
Signal our batteries on the farther shore
To play upon the Fort! Be steady friends—
Be steady! Now upon your country turn
Your multiplying thoughts, and strike for her!
Strike for your distant and inviolate homes,
Perfumed with holy prayer at this hour!
Strike! with your fathers' virtue in your veins
You must prevail—on, on, to the attack!
[BROCK _and forces advance towards the Port. A heavy cannonading from the British batteries.]
Re-enter_ NICHOL hastily.
NICHOL Stay, General! I saw a flag of truce
Cross from the Fort to the Canadian shore.
BROCK. Halt! There's another from yon bastion flung;
And, see! another waves adown the road—
Borne by an officer—what think you, Nichol?
NICHOL Your threats are conquerors! The Fort is ours!
GLEGG. Yes, look! the gunners have been all withdrawn
Who manned the cannon at yon western gate.
PROCTOR. So many men to yield without a blow!
Why, this is wonderful! It cannot be!
BROCK. Say, rather, should not be, and yet it is!
'Tis plainly written in this captain's face.
Officer with flag of truce approaches.
OFFICER. This letter from our General contains
Proposals to capitulate—pray send
An officer to ratify the terms.
[GENERAL BROCK reads letter.]
BROCK. You have a wise and politic commander!
OFFICER. Our General knowing your superior force—
NICHOL. (Aside.) O this is good! 'tis barely half his own!
OFFICER. And, noting your demand of yesterday
With clearer judgment, doth accede to it,
To bar effusion of much precious blood
By reasonable treaty of surrender.
BROCK. Why, this is excellent, and rare discretion!
OFFICER. He fears your Indians could not be restrained.
Our women's prayers—red visions of the knife

CPSIA information can be obtained at www.ICGtesting.com
Printed in the USA
BVOW06s0605030915

416337BV00010B/95/P